ELEPHANT

PLAY

By David Ryals

MAD HATTER
PUBLISHING, INC.

Published by Motor City Press, an imprint of Mad Hatter Publishing, Inc.

For information or bulk purchases:
Mad Hatter Publishing, Inc.
P.O. Box 20973
Ferndale, MI 48220
MadHatterPublishingInc.com

Cover image by Tyler Oberhouse

David Ryals
Elephant Play
ISBN: **978-0-9994692-3-1** (Paperback)
978-0-9994692-2-4 (EBook)

Notice: This is a work of fiction. Although its form is that of an autobiography, it is not one. The characters involved are wholly imaginary. Space and time have been rearranged to suit the convenience of the book, and with the exception of public figures and organizations, any resemblance to persons living or dead is coincidental. The opinions expressed are those of the characters and should not be confused with the authors or publishers.

"All gold rushes are essentially negative." - F. Scott Fitzgerald

"I'm ashamed of it. I'm sick of it. I'm sick of not having the courage to be an absolute nobody. I'm sick of myself and everybody else that wants to make some kind of a splash." - J.D Salinger

"There is not a fiercer hell than the failure of a great object." - John Keats

Chapter 1

Authors never live up to their novels, but I might be the first exception. It's the right thing to say because I definitely sound as good on paper as I do in person. And this novel is as close as you'll get to me beyond the cage bars of my words.

I was born in life's anus. Like me, silent reader, you might have had too many visions of death and violence as a youth. Only then will you think this garbage manuscript, my memories drawn in hot blood, is nothing but pink tea. Hell, it is to me.

All of my short life my mind has been forced to shave the limits to the amounts of agony and violence I can handle. I got so cozy with all the ugly emotions, became such good friends and lovers, that we got married young. No shotgun was needed for our ceremony.

So that's how this new book of mine got written (not published, I assume.) I had blood on the brain since day one. And not just mine. This book, my personalized gift of a non-fiction novel from me to you (whoever you are, silent reader) is not for effect. This book is for a guilt-ridden life of brooding, hard living, constant rejection and a strenuous nervous system wrapped in papier-mâché posturing.

If you knew how well writers act I might be given an Oscar every year. And since my metaphor-parade is underway let me take this fast food bag from your eager hands and enjoy instead the humoring unhappy meal of this novel. Living off of art and poverty your whole life makes you appreciate the things money thinks it can buy. My story shows you don't need digital displays or scented paper to tickle life like a baby.

Early on I knew art is what I would have instead of a life. So I clung to love, hope, humor, and expression – all the things life steals. And I hid my treasures well, well enough to flash your eyes at them and still keep myself and my art.

I'm sure you've seen my hometown floating somewhere on top ten lists of the most treacherous cities in North America and planet earth – I know I have. Last time I checked Baghdad was in better standing. So, I quietly declared, after re-shuffling these injured pages that I loved my trip – my lonely quantum leap from one soiled lily pad to another across an ocean – and this book it birthed more than anything because love on that scale, in this form, can only be shown through an incommunicable gesture like a kiss.

A real kiss says more than all of Shakespeare, but to try and constantly think like that is futile. Revelations and poetry are akin to music - they're a stormy treat for rainy days. So I hope you're in need of a life-altering piece of my most delicious treat, silent reader. We now know all thought is stormy, thanks to the great minds who keep wrestling with the human brain. And since we all came from Africa that means human thought came from there, which means Africa is the mother of our nightmares. Want to know why man is always at war with himself? Look to Africa.

In Africa, the only truth is uniform violence. That's why nature is the most majestic and divine sight because it's the most violent. There's no real law except mayhem and it's eclipsing your face 24/7. You, like me, would come to find justice is a man-made concept.

There's little difference between a jungle, a galaxy or a ghetto. And the parts that follow here are not the domesticated, sunny and humanized universe with all its dark matter, black holes, altering physics, stealthy pigments, rogue asteroids, speculative wormholes and scattered stars etc. Silly things like democratic morals or humanistic regulations cannot breathe in such a bloated, nonsensical environment. I heard an endangered monster's blimpish laughing over there, and now so will you. At the end of my words, you'll be left with the immoral but immortal truth preserved for your amusement. You're welcome, so don't mention it.

I now wager, re-reading this that my home's humorless temperament trying to constantly rape me all my life was awesome training. Oh, I'm laughing now, but only because I'm afforded that luxury – I'm in another land of laughter. Online there was an ad to volunteer abroad. Okay! I stole $950 to get my license to wander overseas. That's the crime I'm guilty of off paper – stealing money to accomplish this novel.

But, honestly, my gestures are always jesting. My looks don't match my personality. My body doesn't match my energy and my actions don't match my behavior. And I am telling you, silent reader, how I love life so much and so often that I live off of my imagining of it. It's hard to explain that to a reader, only writers understand. If you're a real writer life comes to you in drops and you make molten oceans of its potency.

Writing begins where living ends. And I've stopped living again for the moment. A lot of us have. My generation was the first to confuse success with ambition. Quick tip – success is freeing, ambition is confining. But this is what happens when you turn life into a marketplace; some people become worthless and obsolete.

And while I'm a defective product, I'm not without my novelties. Only now after my eyes graze these gnawed pages can I consider forgiving the world for always hating me. The initiator was my dad's heart failure. I won't tempt myself with my wordplay there. It biologically stopped over dinner with his molten red face cushioned in his atrocious pasta – now that that was over - where to go?

My dim tastes reached out over a world map. Dim visions of world cultures and societies spun as a fat happy globe in my muted mind. Where to? It was so well guessed from such unscholarly, informal information – my lifelong education. I knew I'd like this general region of this country or that continent.

Entertainment, politics, art and a few other camouflaged conceptions acted as a travel agent for me. Like education now, it's all do-it-yourself. I paid enough attention to know I liked certain parts of Canada, Mexico, Europe, Asia, Australia, South America and Africa, but, how to decide? Where is fate's magic marker, neon highlighter or sharp virgin dart?

I tossed two old beer caps from my bedroom floor with one hand over my eyes. Kronenbourg landed on Luxembourg and Mr. Artois plopped on Africa. The cast shadow of a spider crawling on the warm twisted bulb above, beaming down his knifing silhouette over Chad Africa, settled it. I'll go where he's going!

I summed as best I could in five minutes why I was off for good to my blank, bloated mother – something about not taking it anymore, etc. I left the note in the mailbox and packed a hand-me-down blue checkered duffel bag with a ream of white paper, one lone pen, few choice books, my plain clothes and hailed five busses to the airport downtown.

All my life I've been waiting for this life-dial to click to the groove I've been priming myself for. I've waited. Oh, I've lost a lot and given a lot and I finally have a lot. For well over twenty years, yes, that's me, I've waited in bus terminals there, train stations here, bedrooms - where?, basements - how?, attics - never again!, parks – with no lovers, forests – with no friends, highways – with no car, restaurants – with no hope, theaters – with no money, schools – with no justice: all inside hell itself. Wow! Finally! Here I am…the last lonely wait with myself at the airport ten miles from my only home.

En route I briefly scrutinized the depleted downtown district. I couldn't feel the sentiment of it being the last time. If I go home again it won't be to another demolished, rolled-over section of America. It's all poor clichés like me; unwanted and struggling for no good reason. I am not just another damn dumb product of my useless fucked over generation.

Back home it had gotten so bad that I only went out with my last friend once or twice a year to a handicapped dance club or dried up dive bar. I couldn't count the hairs on my legs in those bathroom stalls but I can decode the DNA of the universe. Trust me, silent reader, I'm much more ironic than I just revealed.

After two hours and an eventual layover in Zoo York, we hit the island skies of the Atlantic. Now, bidding adieu to America in the form of snarky skyscrapers and claustrophobic cunts scurrying clockwise, I nearly got sick in my little red seat. Not a nauseous sick but a sad sick like when your mother abandons you on your first day of school. I saw and felt those primped people as hard-shell insects clicking and clawing at light speed through brick honeycombs. The speed and sounds made my face dissolve into my stomach and my stomach jump away.

But, the bowed ocean below calmed it all down. It was much more than bugs and boobs but I'll get into that later, much later. There's a reason words like love and loath, life and death, are so familiar with each other.

As a lock tumbler to my sensuality, the hands of love and loath grind and pry me open helplessly. In my brick-hard and brick-red chair, I did something I had checked to do lately – sit alone in public and read, catch up on the world. I politely bothered the stewardess for some copy.

Reclining into my goal I snooped through the papers feeling more individual and complete. Skimming over the obituaries in one local rag from Brooklyn I saw again the memory of my deceased high school crush. After her death three years ago I came across the news in a tacky hometown 'Times' that read,

After her apparent suicide, coroners discovered a tattoo that read, 'To infinity and beyond!'

I chuckled over it again on the plane and here in this loud library just now.

Of course in high school, almost ten years ago, I resembled a titanic mother of forty. But, in my early twenties, I traded in my rose-colored glasses for some sleek new X-Ray specs and every failed novel I wrote was really the blueprint to a meticulous prison break. And, here I am … not because the publishing industry got wise and adopted me but because I seized this initiative and enacted an unforgettable plan B.

And, at twenty when I sprang alive with wordplay and idea-weaving I knew the first blueprint would bring itself to life in my newly hyper hands. The second one would. The third couldn't miss! The fourth was sure fire! … And here is number five.

Much has changed, much was chiseled and replaced. My dead crush never saw the new me. And I saw my life changing again in my seat. I did have the guts to finally create my self-made success story. Hell, I'm almost thirty. I just had to wait to do it right. It's all about luck and timing, I suppose.

Before my farewell, I burned the four unpublished manuscripts in our rusted-out fireplace. Their ashes sleep there today. I contemplated keeping their battered bodies for later tries with publications but I decided it was too much baggage and that if I didn't have enough material to finish my best novel after this was over than I had no business being a novelist anymore. I decided beforehand to make this my grandiose work. And it's strictly autobiographical - how weird for a supposed work of fiction.

There was my cancer-riddled grandmother and her flesh-colored purse. Those are my nimble fingers flipping inside for money. After a month I made a money order out to 'The Avid Africa Foundation' at the corner liquor store. The $950 covered my ticket, two month's stay in rural Chad and food/shelter costs. I forged my application with them – lying again to appear normal and qualified. But the joke and the yoke are on them. I would do my two months of philanthropic service then roam off for good.

I got myself lost in plenty of malls and department stores as a kid with the security guards tripping after my harness, why couldn't I get lost inside Africa? Tossing the papers in the chair beside, I stretched up for the brochure inside my overhead bag. On the cover of the three-fold piece stands a smiling young man attired and hedged to rugged scholarly perfection. His speak bubble should have read, 'My parents loved me too much!' instead of, 'You can be me today!'

I was him now. I no longer desired to be. Now I can take care of myself while I move around inside the successful persons' club unfettered and unsuspecting. They get what I give them. Successful people were always against me. But, my ironic and healthy new adult tact allow me to nestle inside their private club for my guarded amusement at their inhuman and boring transparencies. In short, fuck successful people.

I doubted my camp would be filled with pompous popes like this Mr. Wonderful. Assuming such luxuries should be circumvented before anxieties ruin trips. Ignoring my own guessing I studied the pictures on the pamphlet: a big cool lion roared at the camera in one photo above a promotional paragraph, while skinny loin covered natives danced in the sand and an African bull elephant glared from lush brush on the back.

The titanium skinned hulk and his eight ball eyes were a tad intimidating but in a faraway sector of my fears. My main concerns were people; fitting in, looking good and forging bonds. Yes, those cobalt tanks were loose and it might scare me if I'm alone or stalled in a jeep, but it was speculative and distinctly not-human so I could't get too enraptured.

I had no idea I would see a prize penguin there. I got a two for one deal because elephants and penguins have been my favorite animals since childhood. The animals were going to be bonuses. That's all I could tell in my seat.

I let my nerves soar alongside the sight of the bent ocean. One pleasant thing I encountered was finding elephant poachers understanding of my disdain for traditional zoos while people back home quietly disapproved of my hatred for them. I guess I found killers are more empathetic because they play more than one side.

That's an obvious truth – being two-sided always gives you the advantage. Most people love a touch of ugliness in their beauty and I'm just ugly enough to be gorgeous. Being an outsider in society gives you the upper hand in art if you're an artist. All I'll say now, after all of this, is that my cake is still on ice while its counterfeit brother mumbles in my stomach acid.

Everything I've created here is the sprinkles on my life's dessert. And luckily I found out after I dotted the last period inside this novel while sucking the flavor of life's sugar from my enamel, my sweet tooth never rots. So now you've seen me. You've seen my smile. You've seen my fangs. And you've shaken my claws. And here I am.

Chapter 2

I watched the old black beast rotate by its neck from a railroad crane. It was the color of a tornado in the Tennessee sun. In dreamland, I had recreated the incident I read about years ago in a high school history book that I later destroyed - forever refusing to pay the $75. In my seat, I was with plaid hicks chewing vegetation in a dirt patch watching an elephant twist around like a scary furniture piece in the air.

I saw in that same time, as I read about the elephant hanging down south, Edison's goofy footage of another black elephant frying from the feet up. Seeing disturbed elephants face American justice always reminded me of the speedy colorless scenes showing the Nazi's liquidating books. When stale, pressurized reality greeted me in my seat I checked to see the pamphlet was face up so I wouldn't see the elephant on the back. I hate hearing the songs I dream about when I wake and hate seeing the things I dream of.

The pilot's little, scrambled voice said we would land at N'Djamena International Airport in fifteen minutes. Tucking the brochure into my bag before buckling down, I glanced over the U.S. Department of State's travel warning for Chad they included with my ticket. A typical red flag popped up when the travel agent handed me my travel voucher. It told of indecent behavior and indecent natives inside a decent land.

Skidding passed then rolling towards the sand-faced front of the airport I dropped a spicy red gum stick in my mouth to soothe me. The pack I always choose shows a sugary devil laughing at the chewer. Idling through the terminal I saw only one lone runway strip from the windows. Shining black skulls strode around me. Each meticulously sequenced color pattern weaving by drifted warm new odors.

Two posh young American men barked the head off an elderly black cabbie. He wisely nodded then paused to show them they were wrong and to listen, but they didn't. The buzzing tourists, I'm sure they prefer 'adventurer' or 'explorer', reminded me back home was mainly a titanic clotting of aggravating clowns. When I saw them here, bunched neatly in patches, I saw them as a scattering of privileged harlequins stumbling into another brief act inside their lives' eternal sideshow. ♫♪ Do do dodododo do do do ♪♫

I'm just glad I expend cool resources to keep me looking natural throughout life. I never lose my temper or get out of order when pressed for an exit. I will jump into a burning house before I let myself down by looking and acting silly. My mind and behavior are arranged to my advantage always.

Close bodily scents and the streaming sea of black androgyny lifted my senses up and propelled me forward. I had to pause by the entrance/exit to spot my bus ride to Village Bruno. Outside, scurrying vendors and blathering merchants peddled smoking flesh and counterfeit jewelry around their stands. Their metals rippled and slithered with every move.

I stepped further down the avenue to outrun the murderous odor of smoldering skin. I intentionally glazed over the butchers by focusing on each small pack of people to find my ride. I felt if my pupils dilated on the ghastly meat once more my brain would rupture to compensate. The sizzling curve ahead on Avenue Charles de Gaulle showed my antique bus parked sideways by a grassy island beside the airport.

I gripped my bag to maneuver over. I saw all the vehicles around me, alive and dead, were antiques. Zooming, beeping and gaseous I saw I was now anchored in the third world that trailed seventy years behind the first. I toyed with believing I plunked into an old gangster film about tropical drug smugglers but I dropped the tasteless tease.

Several other volunteers were already on board. Mark Hubble smiled at me from behind the wheel and shook my hand.

"Hi, do you have your passport and papers?" He checked them over while I deflected my discomfort by inspecting my bag, stewing for nothing beside the brick of blank pages.

"Welcome home - I'm Mark Hubble. There are twenty-four people that need to arrive before we leave. You can sit anywhere you want."

Getting gutsy I positioned my bag and myself across from him. "So Mark, are you the leader or…"

He un-tucked his legs from under the wheel showing their basketball length and swiveled towards me, "Avid

Africa has been around for three years. Right now I'm the go-to guy for the founders of the program." He scratched his naked knees then rounded the sweat off his chiseled face, "They know me best because I've come back three times so far. This is my fourth; they give me more responsibilities each time. The natives know me very well by now, too."

Already I caught his selflessness hiding behind no-nonsense goodness. Later on at the village, over many nights of wet liquor tumblers and talks, he would break my heart with stories of others taking advantage of him. When I talked he looked away, always rerouting his pureed thoughts. His busy mind and busy schedule made him impersonal at first but being the stagnant isolated artist who's always sponging off life he came to be my most earnest contact in Africa - proven to be true if you are reading this book, silent reader.

"I read about Village Bruno on the pamphlet. You've been building it for two years now?"

"Yeah, we call them seasons and yeah it has been a ton of work. But it's getting completed this season." Between his sentences he welcomed others stepping into the baking bus. Unlike back home, there were no bugs or mosquitoes in this heat. I came dripping from a crippled swamp and now I'm burning inside a crippled desert.

After enough formalities, not breaking into anything personal, I reeled back to daydream outside the old squared window. Sand kicked up and swarmed the tiny lot. Already some of the young females around Mark and I's age were extending themselves a bit too far to him. He was all bloodless business, though I ignored the business for the blood. He fired up the antique engine and handled the refurbished machine well.

I asked about the steering and it was not powered - his tendons and veins flexing every inch of the ride. We rattled below the Pharaoh's hotel. Junk dealers bargained along the roads with a few typical Mosques' decorating the yellow flat land. Low polite trees and strings of block buildings peppered the rest of the landscape. Down stretching, the rocky brush-stained desert opened up as civilization fell away behind. The flood of motorists was slowly strained to a half dozen.

Roadside, along a cored mountain range, a family of camels and their herders drank from a spring lake. Mark manhandled the big brown wheel onto a well-traveled side road.

Speaking to me from his side, "This is the road to Bruno. We'll be there in five minutes."

I nodded big enough so he could detect it. The suburbs we passed inside N'Djamena could pass for streets in Haiti or any other third world oasis.

Of course, I would have to travel to this place, a place with no immediate conclusions or ready-made answers. But, I reminded myself, discoveries are a drop-by-drop experience, so what I conclude will eventually appear to me and then to you in this book. The bus bumped and bounced hard enough to make some of us vocal about our nerves. My lower back crunched down on a sand hole and I sweated pain instead of fear.

The one name sprouting from the back was Rayless Jester. Over and over and on and on she repeated herself to the audience she drew, "Rayless Jester. Yeah, Rayless Jester, my parents are rich hippies."

Until we parked on the buoyant sand it was all hippies and jesters.

"This is Village Bruno!" Marked scrunched the door free and began lecturing us, them really – he didn't down look to me at his side. "Now, we're centered in a village between four points; East is Lake Chad, South is the capital N'Djamena, further south is Lake Fitri and the only northern city you'll want to go to is Mao – a city slash watering hole."

Gathering by the bus were the curious and happy young Chadians dressed in a mash of Western, Middle Eastern and African fashions. Their speech sloped and curved and I discerned French tongues in their mouths. Another fire stick between my teeth and I was off after the others.

In a swell of happy hot blackness and rainbow swirls the men clamored for our hands. In the rush, I saw few of the volunteers could exchange with them. I was mostly mute to the three men gripping my shoulders and chattering through smiles. I grinned and chattered back the few French words for 'Hello' and 'Thank you' I could remember. The boiling dirt shot up my nostrils inside the vat of eclectic sweat. It was like smelling the kids' playroom at a dirty fast food restaurant in the summer.

We all shuffled to the center of Bruno: the grey brick water well in the village square. Mark was heads above us all and back in business mode. All of the women and children stayed behind the stone wall encircling the square. Their huts were a mix of straw, grass, and wood but the colorful few looked like ocean garbage drugged up and left to cope on land. I studied these garbage igloos through the commotion.

Eventually, Mark and a few male villagers by his side took center stage before the well, "Everybody! Welcome to Village Bruno!" The natives roared a quick victory shout. The mothers among the women bounced and fed the babies in their arms as Mark yelled the itinerary of our new lives. I scanned the crowd and deftly screened his narration. I'm always separating my attention spans.

Camels, llamas, cows, donkeys and human children stood and wormed around. Mark talked of the school we would continue to build and eventually teach in. A new mosque was being constructed here. Five new huts for growing families would be assembled and more farming will be done. But this season the school and the huts were priorities. Other goals were alluded to and I'm still hoping, even after I left Bruno behind in my past, they are becoming a reality without me. The wish for my eerie memory to still be walking among that brave village remains as well. I'm hoping this book is being read by the new students of the new school.

Suddenly I was acutely aware of my gum. Should I suicide-dive it from my teeth or secretly flick it away? I swallowed it until I was sure of an answer for later pieces.

Mark introduced the three young delegates of Bruno as Hassan, Gustave, and Hubert: all lean, all dim, all fathers. They had the flannel candor of young farmhands in my old state. They stood in short-sleeved lumberjack shirts and khakis, barefoot, with the bold blankness of workers nursing humble ambitions.

The only difference I saw between Mr. Smith and Mr. Hassan was nothing. They were all loved and had a place in this world because of enduring concrete traits that live across borders, cultures and other consequential human inventions. The invisible symmetries that bind Mr. Smith and Mr. Hassan across oceans and continents are fundamental grooves in the fingerprints of humanity. There's purpose for me too, the queer grooves that mark the crucial differences for a forensic indictment. But I've finally accepted that love, for me, belongs in science fiction. It was all fantasy and never real.

*****

Rayless Jester preened herself and contorted her body for Mark's peripherals. She stood skinny and curved under the high white sun, posturing with oval shades and a billion dollar grin sparkling against my bankrupted glower. The other girl volunteers were already positioning themselves beside the boy volunteers of their choice. A couple of people I wanted to believe weren't like everyone else showed me everyone is just like everyone else.

Everyone paid Mark mind and acted as though my being was still stuck back home. The ghostly feel of intruding, of being a deserted observer among an unwitting crowd entered and I felt like a phantom eavesdropper. Rayless shined in her short flashy persona while Mark blabbed on. When everyone dispersed I saw I missed most of everything intended and noted to play catch-up later on with Mark.

I just streamed with the volunteers into the open sand beside the huts and few angular stone structures. Mark retrieved tents from the bus's belly and handed them out after he told us to form groups of four. I strolled to Rayless and the girl clinging to her heels. Rayless questioned up to me, her friend's head fixed onto Mark still, "Hi, I was wondering if you know Mark?"

"Is this junior high?"

"I'm just curious, you two seem to be friendly."

"I just met him and we seem to get along so far."

"Okay, well this is my friend Lisa Little."

Little Lisa faced me with a smile – all tiny teeth and huge hair, "Hi!"

I saw Rayless was their mutual mouthpiece, "We wanted to leave home after college. We wanted to travel and thought it's either this or job hunting forever. We can't find the life we want back home so we thought this was the most rewarding option." She beamed her perfect teeth up to me, looking blind behind her shades.

"I'm sure some of the natives would be glad to help you two find your rewarding experience."

Teeth gone, she looked at the rolled orange tent Mark was handing me. He let us know he would stay with us.

Mark knew what was up. He had that gorgeous preternatural artist's perception and it was never lost on me. "I'll help the others and come back."

Rayless jabbed my arm, "so can you pitch a tent by yourself?"

"I did all the time as a kid back home."

At the village square, by the beloved grey well, Hassan, Gustave, and Hubert directed the breezy children back to their huts and the adults to their duties. Some parents left for the wet dykes just beyond the village and their children followed with sticks and stones. The other adults convened inside the half-built, all-age and all-purpose school.

*****

The avocado-green storage doors stayed open under the vandalized crown. To me, it looked half destroyed, not half built. How could it not? This is Chad, this is a natural war-zone like back home. After a certain point, I can't tell what's rotting or growing. Rayless and Lisa parted to one side to let me construct. The soft orange vinyl brushed apart.

I found the tools and accessories tucked in the folds of the tent's skin. Showing off how simple it is to stake four corners and prop the inside with jointed rods, I dared them to help anytime. Of course, they were disinterested and abject to my show of down-syndrome simplicity. I guess having shelter in a desert isn't a rewarding enough option. "Enjoy your new home, ladies."

They started in when I asked Rayless to carry my bag. Speechless and well contained, she complied.

"I'll be back; I'm going to look around." Kicking passed the scarce growths I stood on the worn line dividing Bruno from outer nature. The sand/dirt combination mended under my rubber soles. The earth belonged to the people but the fossilized sand roads and deathless stone in outer orbit belonged to time. Time here wasn't a surreal vortex like a lesser abstractionist might discern it was an elemental force like water.

Time was exhibited inside and outside every natural memento in sight. The sun-fried sands and star-kissed rocks were footstones to everything we cannot control, the one natural resource we cannot harness and manipulate – time.

David Ryals

Death doesn't kill you out there, time just nestles you to its breast forevermore. For now, I chose life and stomped on the so-called stopwatch of the desert.

Before fluttering homeward the reeling pang I held on the precipice of infinity was ghosted by the old emerald parks and white baseball diamonds of my early youth. The sunny scenes knocked my senses around like so many boyhood crushes during so many summers. I looked back and saw Mark scurrying from tent to tent helping others situate. Lisa and Rayless vanished so I lay inside the glowing acrid vinyl.

I saw Mark's sharp sculpted legs step passed the opening of our orange bedroom. My hands cupping my cerebellum I played with what book to read in my bag. The first fetal kicks of this story started in that incubating tent on my back waiting for inspiration to blow its cool unexpected words into my skull. Of course, its first real cries would be heard when this was all over when I could finally retreat to transcribe it from ink to screen.

Mark crawled in and stood on his knees while I sat up, face to naval, and proved my attraction correct, validating my hunch of him as spearhead for my best novel.

"Hey bud, how are you doing in here?"

"I'm a little hungry and thirsty. I almost vomited when I saw the cooked meat outside the airport."

He posed by my side like a cosmopolitan Buddha, "It was pretty rank. You can always fill up a spare bottle or pot with water at the well."

I rotated to him, "Is there anything to eat besides meat? I forgot to take vegetation inside a desert into consideration before leaving."

"Being vegetarian isn't a good idea here."

"Yeah, but being here isn't a good idea. It takes determination to do both."

"It always takes determination to do good things."

"Exactly."

He leaned to remove a trinket form his hip pocket, "Do you know a lot about animals?"

"I know weird random facts and probably not much more than anyone else."

"Can you tell me if it's real?" It dropped from his long veined hand, "The vendors on the avenue see me all the time now and when I first parked at the airport today and stood by the bus a roadside jeweler offered me this for helping out the people so much."

I pinched and turned a beetle-sized sculpture of Chad between my thumb and forefinger.

"Can you tell if it's real?"

"Real what?" I checked the pebbled slab. "It's like carved rock or plaster."

"Smell it." The dangerous waft set off innate alarm bells that hint of blazing bodies.

"It smells like burning hair or burning teeth when you're at the dentist."

"I think it's real then."

"Is it a certain type of rock?"

"It's ivory."

I inspected again, "I can see that. My dad was a butcher and I used to visit him all the time in the meat department at work when I was a kid."

"Yeah?"

"This reminds me of a dead animal, though this is like a death rock, not frozen death like in a meat locker."

"I wouldn't know, what do you mean a death rock?"

"It's frozen but not cold, it's like a death coin or something."

"That's appropriate." Mark reached for it sideways. His newfound gem was handled with invested caution now. "I need to bury this; I can't sell it or be caught with it."

"Can you burn it?"

He brushed his hands off on his shorts, "No, I tried. It just turns black and flakes away." He had to manipulate his frame to be normal in normal spaces. His upper back arched and twisted when he moved closer, "I showed you because you seem level-headed and calm. Don't tell anyone about it okay, even after I get rid of it. We don't need rumors of ivory being handled here."

I loved the way he said he saw me – handsome and poetic. After he and I snaked from the tent he was too determined to slow down for my smaller steps so I double-timed alongside. By the village and sand border, I stargazed as he knelt and clawed three handfuls of khaki earth and pressed the little dead moon in its grave.

"The thing was appropriately carved but it's too risky to keep around." We stood talking to the meridian.

"What's appropriate?"

"Chad. The ivory trade is thickest here. Most of all the ivory in the world is siphoned here." Dusk's sun splashed luminous blood and shadows across the ancient land. Hollow rattles burst faraway, spurting and stopping.

"Is that machine gun fire?"

Mark and his cool, skatepark voice explained it was happening all over Chad now. If gunfire is close, hide. If gunfire is far, run. The 50th Anniversary of Chad's independence was upon everyone. As the day lost its power the night released its charge. Behind in Bruno few villagers kindled fires around their garbage igloos. Light, broken chatter hit and missed us.

"When you have to use the bathroom at night take a flashlight with you because lizard life and other creatures come out and wait for you. I have a few in my bags I'll lend to the tent.

"What's the scariest thing you've encountered in the night here?"

He rotated towards Bruno, "I stepped passed an elephant in the dark, blindly. It gave its trumpet wheeze and I fell over. I couldn't breathe for a minute. I was lying in the sand with the tarantulas and snakes."

Professional and calm he took the lead back to Bruno. Back home, gunfire typified reassurance and relief. Nighttime gunfire is only the cruel symphonic crickets to the soundtrack of my life. I skipped beside Mark envisioning the two classmates I went to school with who were shot dead outside the nightclub I briefly worked at. Home, for me, is where the heartless is.

Suddenly, I grew glad I wasn't in portentous old Europe. I thrive with gun toting fools. I flourish inside this idiot's bankrupted world. I like to live down, not up – while maintaining my intellect and artistry for my intimate indulgence. Occasionally I flex my brain to show rough-edged clowns, my people, who I can really be and what I really am.

Lisa and Rayless were chatting inside and I saw they had let their hair and breasts down to prepare for the first sleep.

"Where were you?" Rayless asked.

Mark tossed a slick lie without trying, "We went out sightseeing, how about you?"

They yammered on about all the things he first found here with him placating them until their breath ran dry. After inflating the tent with enough excitable talk they eventually zipped the vinyl wall between us.

"I'm going to check on the villagers and see who needs what." The world sheathed his shadow. The girls' static whispers finally cut off and I let the crackling silhouettes from the fires take me away to dreamland again. I woke in the night to the whimpering of one of the girls. I heard the other giggle through her nose. Her nose huffed as the other cried herself to sleep.

Chapter 3

"Because of my decision to be myself, a writer, which is just another word for starving artist today, I was made to feel dead to the world by everyone in it. And in so many ways I am now."

"I thought artists were lively people? And you don't look like you're starving."

"I'm most alive when alone, like any real artist. When someone loves me I know I did something wrong. If people don't hate me or are indifferent I get very uneasy. And believe me, I've starved. I've suffered in so many ways I can't begin to communicate it, at least not with talking."

"That is strange to want to be hated always. And suffering is a privilege. Most people here don't have the luxury of complaining about their suffering. I can tell you're American."

"Well, all Americans my age love complaining but I'm different. And I want people to love my writing, but hate me. It's easy when you've been hated and forgotten all your life."

"Well, I'm glad you've found time to help us with all of your suffering and forgetfulness."

The head honcho of the fathers, Gustave, and I drank warm rusty well water by the half-demolished school. I rapped my knuckles on one green storage door as we found the words we knew to make simple yet weighty chitchat. Talking to a young yet mature foreigner was painful for placid and glassy dialogue.

I guess like art, communication needs to be half obliterated in order to mend the gap and then some to say anything new. But my guest seemed intent on criticizing yours truly and spotlighting the village rather than make any attempt at sympathy. His head shined a blackness akin to a prized Dia De Los Muertos wax skull – the best in the shop. His baby-blue plaid work shirt opposed his complexion nicely. I began to see the villagers needed his attention always. He kept calling back in French to a few distant kids clamoring for his attention.

Whether smart or dumb, right or wrong, he was at least like every other decent man in the third world – mature. "How come you chose to talk to me?" I posed my fingers for respect.

"You look serious."

Hassan and Hubert kicked around nearby, snooping on us. Finally, they settled by my sides waiting to interrupt at a weak spot but they dared not interrupt Gustave clumsily.

"Your face looks like you think too much." He furrowed his features to a gremlin's grimace.

"I've seen too much life." I put on a stinging grin, giving him my version of a wise mocking mask.

"Habibi?" Gustave's face returned and he leaned into Hassan's mouth. After his critical questions, Gustave informed him in choppy Arabic.

I saved an inspired line for him when he turned to me again, "I'm at that age where you can live off of life and nothing else."

He opened his lips and paused, showcasing his amused smile, "Not here, baby."

I coiled one brow.

"Hassan and the others say they want to gather everyone and begin today's work. Please tell Mark to gather his people here at the school and we will divide everyone into different areas that need work done. You can live off of work now." Before leaving, his calloused charcoal hand patted my sharp shoulder. Kids conferred and darted around my legs. But they all gravitated back to their approaching satellite – Mark Hubble.

"Okay, so do you know how to mix cement? Or mold bricks? Or do you want to unload the straw from the bus and fix some of the huts?" The three village leaders were already operating behind us.

"I'll work on the school with you."

"I'll gather up everyone else from our group."

Quick, excited shrieks rang from the ground when the mother's whispered what was happening into the children's ears. The men, mobilizing at the school, nudged the kids aside and warned them away. When the villagers and volunteers rustled the earth kicked up and danced with them. A dirt fog rose high around the children.

Hassan and Gustave uncovered the encrusted cement mixer and pushed it towards one side of the school. I just tagged with Mark until someone told me my duty. Mark eventually handed me a spare pair of rumpled gloves. As my hands slipped and fit them on I spotted and swiped a trowel and waited for the men to stop mixing the mortar.

French words peppered us in this worker's bath and I could do nothing but feign normality in the absurd spot. I could emulate normalcy by sniffing out and imitating their simple culture and simple candor. Splat, scrape, smooth – the trowels at play scratched my nervous system raw.

"Aidez-vous maintenant, votre imbécile!" A villager jutted to the moldering wall with his head.

So I joined the group, slipping heavy dark mortar along the ledge of dusted bricks. Two men swung a brown tarp off the brick mountain imported from town last season. A few old villagers in summer colors crept far outside us, scrutinizing our muddying labor. The young villagers minded the concrete and mortar with Mark and me while the volunteers handed off bricks in a cartoonish factory fashion.

Sensing a tiny oddity somewhere, I peeked back to see a few women volunteers standing apart watching us, then head for shelter inside their tents. The village of orange vinyl resembled a suburban frontier in the African nether-land.

"When did you learn to lay bricks?" Mark muttered to me at my side, him straining beside me with growing clay hopping from his body to mine. "I always did odd jobs back home. I had to lay brick, mix cement, cut and stack wood and butcher deer during hunting season. You can't get away with not using your hands back home."

Silence was followed by a deep flat, "Yeah..."

I always opposed my statements against my ears, every one, and I couldn't immediately figure his detachment with what I said. Eventually, I found Mark to be too upstanding to stray from his duties. He never elaborated unless he had the time - forever putting work before pleasure. Only brimming glass tumblers and long night talks unlocked the vault of his terminal angst.

Like me, dozens of invisible lasers were constantly tripped by his sensitivities, warning him to recoil and lock himself down at the threat of an intruder prying for honest answers about himself or his tragically worshiped parents - in particular, his father. It was eventually revealed that those two figures were his hidden idols of faith. And like all idols, they stunk of hypocrisy and deceit.

But household religions have no place in my space. For now, I just kept eyeing his inner museum up close and afar. The tone of the kids' ruckus shifted and a few of us leveled our eyes to the village. A tiny, tranquil sand-colored elephant settled near a cluster of straw huts. Gustave and Hassan nudged their heads for each to go over. I shuffled my eyes between the concrete and the curious kids.

Gustave patted the virgin beast's jowl as Hassan slapped its rear to move ahead. Naturally, the children followed until the elephant reached us. By now I discerned when the lesser known and seldom used Arabic was spoken it meant business between those who understood it – the somewhat educated and therefore more important ones. I heard Gustave and Hassan share some as they approached. A few men motioned us aside while Gustave and Hassan guided the creature through the open doors.

Hassan spanked the baby beast onward inside the school. Gustave rejoined us to brush the kids back. Gustave quickly stepped out and locked the doors when a hollow thunder sounded close by. The mothers whisked their kids inside their huts. I knew that thunder.

It showed itself as the hoofs of horses. Well-armed rogues were violently summoned into Bruno. Their swift explosive presence was frozen by a phantom control, leaving a bright sand cloud speeding beyond them as they spurred their horses. A dreamy malice invaded our atmosphere.

Over a decade of relentless news coverage of terrorism back home made my blood pump hard when they appeared. Four sat sturdy and serious. That goofy ambiguity before a fight or a kiss encircled the village.

The centerpiece, the apparent leader, ticked his stud a few steps forward with his clicking tongue. I checked Gustave but his features showed that disarming naiveté that the wiliest men play. The male villagers moved forward enough to make a silent statement. Wrapped in creamy dusted clothes, anchored in brown military boots and crowned with a shemagh turban, the man smiled behind his thorny black beard. He pushed the strap of the AK-47 further up his shoulder, "يأتون إلى هنا !مرحبا."

Gustave met him halfway and loosely replied. The man's theatrical sighs of understanding held us on high alert. His close cronies wore rifles and sub-machine guns on themselves. A mother's garbled demand shot from a hut when a child popped from its entrance to shoot a pebble at the man's ear. He didn't acknowledge the stone. He kept speaking undisturbed.

Disciplinary slaps from mama ricocheted through the square as Gustave and the man jawed. I envied the boy because I at once wished I had a used sex toy to hurl at his face – a rubber penis right across his rotten mouth, for I heard the word "Elephant" in his exotic English then "الفيل" in his suave Arabic. I fumed alone in my spot, feeling for the animal in the school.

Gustave dimly shook away his inquiries before they shook hands and stepped apart. As a single entity, the gang galloped back south with that silent procession of their fiery horses. Gustave collected Mark, Hassan, and Hubert. Us others broke apart to continue the construction as they huddled in ardent secrecy. We heard the baby beast start huffing dirt around inside the blasted building when we began again.

Now the 'E' word emerged inside the addled sounds of our work. The men discussing the poachers shook their heads mournfully while sloshing and scraping the soft stone. I liked the soft stone best. I preferred the sensual mortar in the aesthetic contest in my muddled mind. It was sleek, young and soft opposite the dry blocks of matured heaviness.

Lost in my thoughts Mark scuttled back up beside me, "I got rid of the pendant just in time."

"They wouldn't have found it or smelled it on you, those fucking clowns."

Mark, searching for a decent reply, worked quietly beside me for a whole minute. "No. But I got rid of any chance of anything happening. They wanted to know if that little elephant they spotted had its family here too. Gustave lied. He said it was alone and must have strayed from its family. He said now that they've spotted an elephant around here they want to make their presence known to the village. Gustave said he heard about these people a couple years ago."

"Where are they from?"

"Somewhere between the borders of Chad, Cameroon and the Central African Republic. He said they want to be the village's friends and hopes we can do business with them in the future."

"How?"

"Tipping them off about anti-poaching teams moving around and any elephant activity nearby in return for goods we need and protection."

"They're just terrorists. All villains pretend to be your friend to get you to sign an unfair contract until death."

"Yeah, we're not challenging them, we just don't want trouble. Gustave just placated them so they'd leave. I don't think he seriously wants them around, but who knows. I hope he doesn't."

Mark and I shut up when we saw a hundred eyes listening and passively engaged. At night our modest achievements showed through the tent opening from my back atop a two-inch mattress of rubber composite. The side view of the school was being tucked in for the night by the dusk. The intimate fires inside and outside each hut would soon flare. Already the children played by the school.

I watched the other kids, the ones slightly older than me, peel towards the school at the end of my busy street as a toddler. I didn't know then that things of promise and beauty seldom achieve the expectation of their allure. It's the ugly, easily dismissed refuges that hold the most personal gratification and reward for me. Older now, much older, I hoped the kids in my sight wouldn't become me.

I begged not one of those kids to be like me, I wanted them to have it better. They don't deserve to know that a traumatized mind makes all aspects of life more unbearable than the worst physical suffering imaginable. If you're mindless you're already home-free, nothing can hurt you too much when you have no concept of anything outside your limitations.

They played while I hoped. The men spluttered unevenly in the dark by the desert, along the main road to Bruno. A low fire appeared and danced at their legs. Gathering my sources I stretched out and left to join them at the fire. At certain points, I saw through the dome of Africa's sky the glittering guts of our galaxy spattered along a winding horizon.

"Drink, Please!" Hassan slung a sparkling bottle of Francis' Gin at me. Uncorking it I downed two mouthfuls. Immediately Hubert, the runt, passed a fresh jug of Arak to my palm: the grape diesel drink of back home. When 150 proof spirits slid down my throat and cannonballed the sulfuric acid in my stomach I heaved away the fumes for hot breaths.

"It's good?" Hubert slurred his best, inviting me to join. "Yes…is this from N'Djamena?"

He steadied himself, "This? No. This is from Ali. He gave it to us men."

Alpha leader Gustave edited Hubert's spill, "Ali is the man who stopped by earlier. He assures protection and much-needed commodities for information."

"And a place to hide."

"Well – place to stay when he needs it. French troops in Mao and N'Djamena get this special and sell it to the natives for other things."

"Such as?"

"Mostly physical things."

"Ah."

Mark and Hassan's talk was growing more heated, showing hard lined faces sweltering behind the fire. Hubert poked my elbow to joke about something serious, "In Liberia, this Arak would cost one five-year-old!"

My endurance, being outsourced to cope with this dope's joke, would stay because of the hellish reinforcements built back home. Hell always waves at me. I had to consciously remind myself hell is hell no matter the different breeds.

Gustave studied the fire, bemused at the ugly truth Hubert splashed on us, probably thinking of his own kids playing at school with Mark as its first headmaster. Mark and I could teach the adults and children of Bruno the entire world ten times over. The catch was to dribble it in ways that get them pleading for more and more. I would use the sand floor of the school as a stage for my performances as a parental piper and enchanting enlightener.

Chad's night gusts cradled traces of cosmic freeze, whisking our clothes and burning our skins as it careened through space. The heat-swell of liquor hugged my innards together and reminded me I'm safe if I'm all I have. The night's natural sleep mask approached fast, so soon even the faint smear of horizontal rock would leave us. The medium fire screamed upward, leaving its kind residual effects.

Back home the quick consuming of top-shelf spirits would end quickly with a remorseful blackout. But this was the start of a new season in hell – how marvelous to find heaven in a bottle already.

"I wish for bigger crops and smart children." Hassan rotated around us, trailing off in French.

Gustave snatched the jug from him and patted its base, "Mark, I wish to grow as tall as you. I wish to get sick people healthy here at home…do you know of a wish?" With a melted grin, he handed me the jug and stood baited.

"I wish to help bring peace and happiness to everything here through my work and art."

Slugging the last swallow all of the others studied my wish at the flames. Hubert's first giggles caught fire and a firecracker reaction rang around me. I showed a smile of fake humiliation to get along, to get by without taking a serious tally for silly requital. A drunken vacuum returned in a snap then broke again with another Gustave question, him now fancying me as his comedic barrel of rich fortune cookies, "What are you thinking about now?!"

"Forbearance and counterplay."

Enter Act II of our stupor's silence. When enough crackling and whooshing permeated our company I chucked the sad dry bottle by its erotic neck with a side-pitch into the hidden world.

"Hey! In the morning you'll find that and let us reuse it for the village!" Hassan and his swarthy snootiness snapped at me across the wheezing inferno.

"Sure, I'm sorry I didn't know."

I fielded another Gustave jab, "What were you thinking about when you threw it?!" He smiled into the flames, genuinely pleased he could play on my decency.

"Tell me, Gus, do you really consider Ali a friend of you and Bruno?"

His amusement dispersed, "No, but he would be a better fake friend than true enemy. I humor him and he leaves trouble alone for us."

"You know he will eventually pluck Bruno bone-dry when success comes to the village. He'll ask for more than he gives. And it will be your fault in the end for dealing with a devil and thinking it was innocent."

"I will deal with him, you won't. For someone who's never been here before you talk like you know Bruno so well. You know the men who hunt poachers? Sometimes they stop by here and I lie and say no poachers are around so they don't bring trouble either. Not everyone who wants to do good things brings good things with them. People like Ali are not too bad if you can handle them. I'm prepared to handle anything to keep Bruno safe."

"Would you kill them?"

"Yes."

No retort sprung forward to chase away the Wild West notion here. No one tended the fire so the flames had run away for the night. Dull orange and hot blue slithered on the busted coals.

"Tomorrow will be a new day and a better day."

Hassan assured against the gusts, followed by Gustave's, "And a much better night!" his forefinger tapping the empty bottle. "I bought three bottles in town, just for the week we began. Later, we buy wine when it is finished."

I tried leaving a good impression of myself before I shut up, "What will we do with the elephant?"

Mark hopped on, "I think one of the girls is a veterinarian so we'll see what she can do."

Gustave annexed his reply, showing absolute authority and better judgment, "We keep him here. We will call the National Elephant Monitoring Service in town or we can call a ranger at Zakouma National Park to come get him after the school is finished."

Gustave's velvety French accent cuddled his every letter. He splashed sand with one foot to kill the coals. Pacing myself as Mark and I closed in on our tent I heard him call behind, "We'll look at the elephant tomorrow and see if we can feed him or something..."

"Good. I don't want to see it suffer. It's already lost its family."

Having readymade excursions for the days to come eased the grief of being adrift with myself; it really did shave the edge off. Somewhere in the night, Hubert's screams visited the village. His polyester pants scratched by the well – him jumping, swiping and panting.

At the sun's first peek over the low range bluffs beyond Bruno, superbly melted to the desert floor from time, he regaled us at the school of a snake in his hut. He told us in three languages. The scary serpent was never seen again, but the snake kept blabbing about his fear and surprise well into the workday.

Chapter 4

The children couldn't peek over the high busted walls of the school so some stacked themselves foot to shoulder to catch quick sights of the baby elephant. The less ambitious boys just stood by the drying walls and made noises at it while the girls hushed them to listen in on its cranky racket. I studied them from my side through the tent opening while shirtless Mark scrubbed his big teeth over a brown coffee mug of well-water, his milk tempered pecks twitching with every stroke.

I levied my talk until his spitting was over, "They know how to take care of the elephant don't they?"

"Yep, it's like taking care of a horse in Nebraska; everyone knows how to nurse animals here."

"Its tusks aren't big enough yet to be desirable?"

"Uh, I'm not sure. I don't think so. I wouldn't worry about it."

"I used to nurse squirrels and rabbits back home. I would feed them peanuts and scraps every morning. It's a shame I can't do it here."

Marked gutted his wallet, looking beetle-browed at the bills boasting portraits of gloomy peasants against colorful cultural backdrops. I think our money back home should have abandoned houses and sex organs inked on it. My messy ape-chest snagged the kid's and the women's attention while I drew up water from the stone well from the old wet bucket for my chipped mug.

A girl toddler stamped inside my shadow and pointed, speaking micro French, to my torso. She dipped her forefinger in my water when I offered it to her and few women chuckled behind their hands.

Chadian mornings rushed to my toes, shot up to my sternum and hurried through my scalp. The sun, nature's mother, drowned me in newborn heat and ventilated me with bright virility.

Every morning I was a speechless sprite. My alarm was me rolling around in a burning phantom's embrace until I gasped awake. But outside I always saw myself pouting coolly like an iconic actor placed on commemorative stamps.

There was Rayless standing among the unzipped orange tent colony hunched over her black phone under the beating sun. I noticed the girls, even when transplanted into the wilds of Africa, took longer to wake for the world.

"I never did find out what you did back home. What special qualifications do you have that brought you here?"

She brushed the screen with her thumb over and over, her shades fixed down to the glaring toy, "I'm an R.N."

"How long did it take to become a nurse?"

"I'm not getting any signal here…um, almost five years. I graduated last fall from Ohio State but there were no jobs there and I couldn't network for shit so…I just decided to get more experience for my resume. It'll look a lot better for me when I apply again. "

She capped her kindergartener's spiel with that all smug, all awkward and all nervous smile. Her upper-middle-class persona of pasty privilege made me nauseous if I gazed at it too long. Her five-foot body repelled me like spoiled milk. And I'm sure I repelled her like a bull in a china shop. Heaven forbid I step onto one of her priggish landmines and prompt a pompous reaction.

Her thin lips, evening hair, pancake makeup and humorless irony could have plumbed the robust chambers of my spinster's heart, but the melted scar tissue was too lewd for her ambition. From the start, already at the end of possibilities, we could sense our scar tissue and retreat to our far buried turrets. "The rust belt is a belt full of notches and we were living inside one."

"Where are you from?" Pose for me and the curious world. But after I revealed where I originated from she gave her condolences.

"Hey, be thankful I'm not from Pakistan."

"You know what they say in Pakistan?" Tilt your hip that way, thank you. "Be thankful you're not from *there*."

Slipping her phone into one back pocket, outlined between jean and butt, I decided to play with her. I suppose it was out of boredom with her more than curiosity about her.

"I'm good with construction and hunting. I've been telling all the natives how I'm good at fixing things and good with animals and how I used to hunt them back home when I was younger, but never again. I'm a working class fix-it guy with a bloodhound's nose and philanthropist's heart." I didn't mention my scientific ingenuity and artistic creativity; I didn't want to overwhelm her.

"Why don't you hunt anymore?"

"I became a vegan. I can't stand the idea of killing anything again. It has a lot to do with my dad - he was a butcher. And I don't want to go into it."

"That's fine. Have you done volunteer work before?"

"I've done volunteer work, back home, at animal shelters but never went to school for it."

"Does your dad take care of animals when he's not killing them?"

"He was only a butcher. He used to make me process deer, pigs, and cows with him at his work. He died right before I came here."

"How?"

"Heart attack. Because of him, I became a vegetarian fifteen years ago. I can't imagine being like him ever again. After I wasted my teens brooding and hating him I decided I didn't ever want to be like him. After I grew up, I got it in mind that I should take it further and help other people for once." Grateful for getting my fill she shifted the subject, "You might get to help animals again if this little elephant needs to be taken care of. I like his little tusks. They look like white baby carrots."

We stared at the children, pondering our next move. "I don't want to seem condescending but being a nurse is much worse than cutting meat. A lot of guys get defensive when I bring it up – that I've done things they couldn't."

"You're right, I couldn't be a nurse. Helping my dad cut apart and process dead animals nearly destroyed me as a kid, among living where I lived. I couldn't revert back to trying not to have a conscience about horrific things like death, suffering or torture."

"I can see that. All of the death and suffering I've been around has been natural, though that doesn't make it easy. It isn't perverse like a slaughterhouse must be."

Tossing her a scrap of acknowledged defeat I trailed off with, "Oh, I'm *sure*...".

"Do you want to go over and look at the elephant?" I nodded and she led the way.

Where, for some reason, the kids laughed at me, they shut up and gawked when Rayless strode through the camp. The fossilized instinct of messing with girls to get attention shone in some boys but none had guts enough to prod Rayless. I stacked a few cinder blocks for her to step on while I stood beside, eventually joined by some hesitant children.

The baby beast was the same brownish orange as matured cannabis hairs. My mind hatched the idea of one of those sappy psychedelic strands ballooning into this elephant.

"I wonder where his parents and family are." A mother joining us from behind inquired in the low tonal voice all third world women have; accented, deep and sensual. Obviously, it was the start of her most honest attempt at bleeding us for later indulgence at the rumor mill. Rayless was much more denuded and apathetic to her than I.

I unleashed my social skills and spoke for us both, "Is this very common to get orphaned elephants here?"

"It's getting more common. It depends on the time of year but the poachers are breaking the families apart." She moved in closer and blew off some dusted rubble on the wall between our shoulders. "You men are doing a fine job with the school. The children are all thankful. And I thank you very much."

Her rundown roadside sandals brushed away stray pebbles by the wall, already curating the gift. Her feet were ashy and calloused but the skin shining outside the delicate cloth of her candy-blue and cotton-white summer dress showed in the shade a curvaceous bowling ball of strong, sleek proportions. The women of Chad, especially this one – Gustave's wife, Nya, and indeed all the women I encountered in the third world, had not the giddy goofiness of so-called civilized women à la Barbie and her pink adventures of penis and plastic.

Nya, as she greeted us with a lengthy and healthy hand, was born of and married to the earth. The glee and spirit she showed when chasing the children around showed me there was no deeper beauty than the natural earth and its unruly sprouts. It's how I feel about us being birthed from the universe(s), as you'll read later. Her nail bleeding work in Bruno scoffed at bloated superficiality. Yes, as she later told me, her kind knew better than all others that love replaces what pain steals. And she was prettier and nobler than any queen in any castle when she toiled in the sun.

"Sometimes elephants cry when they get lost from their family. They cry a lot. They're very smart so they mourn like we do. I see it more because of what's happening to them."

Nya, the adult to make me feel clownish and spurious at my best, informed as Rayless and I molested the wall in intimidation. "We can only release him if his family comes back for him or if another family will take him."

"I heard something about national park rangers coming for him?"

"Sometimes when we get an elephant, when they get lost here or in another village, they will show up and take it. Sometimes they lose the elephant."

"Why?" Rayless stared quietly and the brown baby slouched in the corner.

"Because either poachers kill the rangers or bribe them." She swiftly departed with two of the five kids at her side.

Rayless lifted her shades to the baby, "I wonder what he eats?" "They're vegetarians too."

"Yeah - why did I ask that?"

"..."

"Are you and the men working today?"

"You know it."

"I think a few of us girls are looking after the sick kids today and we'll go into N'Djamena for supplies." Prepping to depart she untucked her phone, "Do you want your picture taken with the elephant?"

"Sure."

She sized us up and tapped the screen. "I'll look for some veggies for him in town." She wondered up to me, "If they have any wine or drinks in town do you want me to get some for later?"

"Yeah, that'd be nice."

"Okay."

After she breezed away I felt a rogue electrode leave my heart and zip through my blood. I was shocked by her twin charm, an unsuspecting charm she held that stunned even me. I glimpsed at how Mark could find her as attractive as me. But she didn't win me over with wine. I'm not that cheap and easily buzzed.

After she and a few girls zoomed off through the sand on Bruno's old Japanese dirt bikes I checked today's itinerary with Mark at our tent. "School first, town second, then lunch, back to the school, dinner and maybe playtime." His scowl stayed put as he combed out the gunk from yesterday's hair.

"I'm going to feed the elephant when Rayless gets back. Is there something up?"

His voice rolled out in low tide, "Uh…just a little homesick. None of us get much signal here. The government keeps promising they'll eventually build towers close to Bruno so all the villages nearby can get a signal. We still have to go into town to call and text. It's really nothing to get upset about."

"Than what are you really upset about?"

His words washed away for the big confessional crash, "…that Rayless girl, I think I'm starting to really like her. I want to get us alone so we can talk more." And right then I unearthed my mental measuring tape to mark the heart-broken half-life of the aftermath.

"You really like her like you want to date her?"

He stumbled with his stubble, clicking the single blade razor against the chipped washbowl, "Yeah...she's really great. I think she's great."

I lament, even in those I love, my generation for not being able to talk well. We don't talk in complete sentences and I loathe us as much as I love us for it. "Do you have anything set up?"

He clinked while talking. "Not yet...uh, I'm sure we'll get drinks in town this Sunday. You can come if you want. I've wanted to get all the volunteers together for a group hang out some night this week."

"We'll see what I'm doing."

"Hey, check by the grain houses and see if the women are going to need any help with the dykes before we start on the school."

Under his glue-white flesh, his wing bone shifted beside the heavy protrusion of his vertebrate. I watched his back until I exited, silent. Midget fidgets trembled deep in me with asking the herd of women if they needed help. I sought Nya from the well but she was lost somewhere in the distance or in a garbage igloo.

They were congregated by the grain houses and I strolled over calmly, looking beyond them, "Hi, do you need any help with the crops or farming before I, we, work on the school?"

Fawn eyes and still mouths watched me when I spoke. "Non merci."

Nodding, another woman waved my attention away and rubbed one of the three square clay houses, the grain crypts. Their aesthetic appeal to me was in not appearing to hold the health of hundreds, but the treasures and corpses of forgotten royalty. Those mini pueblo houses of sandy clay that will outlive us all, except me.

She waved me away, pantomiming as best she could that there were enough women for their work and for me to go away. I wandered to the school and perched ten feet away from the baby, the pure and tired lashes batted while its wet eyes daydreamed beyond its confines. Like me, it sat upright on its rear and our thick skin brushed along the impacted earth and manmade concrete as we shifted for comfort.

I couldn't find it in me to scrutinize or assess this creature. A potent but shapeless fear cuddled me as I felt its glare with my peripherals. It felt like I was waiting in the principal's office with the kid I just victimized, but whom I really loved. I didn't want him to hate me for experiencing the worst of me.

My fear edged on wonder: is it mad at me? Will it attack me? Does it want to be loved? I guess it's how people might see me if they saw a certain part of me shine through.

Desperately I wanted to embrace him, but I took him for someone like me and it would have to be absolutely mutual before we could show true affection. We're too touchy to risk our hearts on a hope. I just stayed silent and played it safe.

The farting motorbikes plowed back to Bruno. The beast and I waited in what we hoped would become the dunce's corner. "…I said this was for us. Where are you?"

"Here I am." The doors swooshed open a half inch above the dirt. Her naked stomach and thigh gap oppressed me when she tramped to my cozy head, leaving them in my face.

"It's not enough but I just want to see if he'll eat it first then we can get more."

"I hope we can use the grain in the silos."

"I'm not sure. Here," Puckering up in a carnal crouch she pulled the lettuce heart like a rabbit from a hat and teased the baby's worming snout. It caressed her silk-thin forearm and strangled the white heart into its latex-looking mouth. Chomp, crunch, chomp. "Good, here…" The process repeated for three more hearts.

I interrupted, "What about his name?"

She fondled his trunk, "I'll bring it up to the women and the girls and see what they think. But I want to name him."

"I'll ask the men about the grain so you don't have to keep doing this."

"I had to spend almost twenty-five dollars for those. The price for good food here is outrageous."

"That's why I'm asking about the grain."

"I want to feed him with you if they say he can eat it."

And with that admission, her scent cut into my senses leaving the depressing smells of dirt, greens, and shit to the birds. As a cunning adult, she smiled like a child to the cute and clueless creature, and then looked back to the elephant. I joined-in to pet his stunted tusks that looked like two vanilla ice cream cones. His head bobbed low with humiliation inside our close attention.

"He likes it."

"He does." All this innocence sparking between us for the first time and she had to crash my gears on the floor with shoving her hands in my hair and rubbing my scalp as a crazed sibling would.

"Alright…"

"I didn't have enough for any wine so if you go into town get us some and we'll drink with him tonight." Denuded and dumb from the ditzy powers of shapely fascination I agreed on cue. In Bruno, we always skipped breakfast for work then collapsed into lunch, just like now. Hello boys.

*****

"I don't want to eat here today. I want to go to into town for dinner."

"Are you asking Rayless and Lisa too?" Mark cautiously repositioned a few spare cinderblocks, structuring them further away from the side wall we finished today. Tomorrow the back wall would be built up. His being a math whiz and an architectural savant made disbelief anchor my jaw to the ground. I will forever feel like an obvious tag-along in every situation, but I masquerade my ignorance so well that no one would ever guess my true feelings.

His skeletal digits scratched the dimensions down for the next wall and I peeked to see his notebook filled with ink and graphite sketches of the entire school both individually pieced and entirely completed. I didn't ask if he studied math and architecture and everything else I didn't. He talked while drawing, "I'm not too good with installations, do you know how to install wiring and plumbing?"

"If there's a good hardware store around here - yes."

His humility rode in to save my dignity, "I worked for a short time in a hardware store and picked up a lot of repairs and installations. We would need a water and electric supply. I'm sure the well could be annexed to the school and other buildings made here." But his attention, trapped inside his blended thoughts, was back at the chalky blocks with the notebook fashionably rolled inside his back pocket. "Are you interested in what I said?"

"Maybe, we'll see. I've been thinking about a lot lately." My blood vessels rocketed hot adrenaline through themselves, causing my face to clench into stone. These touchy impasses – do I keep playing the rat's role or impress him by revealing I'm a human mole? "Did I ever tell you I was a writer?" "Maybe."

My lungs, on instinct, sighed for the quick haul, "Yeah, I started my fifth novel here…well, I'm penning it in my head and I'll probably start writing it tonight." And I did silent reader. I knew too well the social hexing I imposed on myself with that gross admission so I had to flush away the stigma. "I think this will be my best work by far. And with this story, I hope to finally get published. Before my father died my grandmother passed away from cancer and whenever I brought it up they were always concerned about when I'll get a real job."

His distractions finally made way for me, "…um, how long have you been writing?"

"Almost a decade now."

"…um, what kind of person was your grandmother?"

"She was a silly old lady with a wicked sense of humor. It took her six years to finally kick. Her life was that of fiction. But I'll see what happens with this novel."

"I'm sure we won't add any plumbing or wiring to anything now because we're not connected to a big enough water or electrical source. You know, just come with me to dinner and then all four of us can go to lunch tomorrow."

"I wanted to walk around N'Djamena and get familiar with the town on my own."

"Sure, we can walk down the main avenue after dinner." I still looked at Mark Hubble as an attractive rival at this point. It wasn't until after his spilled guts lay steaming at my toes that I reconciled his being a good person but a shitty friend because of his poorly hidden troubles.

I could happily accept him after deciding who my first reader should be. When the ugly truth of his own hell back home manifested itself for me, the moment his familial Rubik's cube unlocked itself in my mind, I saw the complete portrait of a permanently shattered man inside a pristine mannequin. But being cursed with a good person who is a shitty friend is draining, especially during the feeling-out process - before you know it's all doomed to fail.

"As long as we're going out somewhere I'm fine." I had to cork our wobbly session. As the baby slept soundly in the hollow spot, the few stray men taking aimless walks in the dusk headed to their huts. "Rabbit, where are we running to for dinner?"

"There's a bar on De Gaulle called the World Away Bar. It's the Chadian equivalent of a hipster bar."

I wanted to throw one last jab before we went to work, "Has anyone approached you about playing basketball?"

"Oh, god…"

The few other volunteers moving in the shirking sun showed to be part of a world I had little to no experience in, the absent T of my life – the upper class. They were purposefully rugged vacationers looking to either cleanse or create their character with volunteer work; engineers for Chrysler, Ford and GM – the three stooges of my home, doctors and dentists, a defense attorney and one struggling middle-aged gym owner.

No, I didn't hear about the score in the football game. No, I don't have children. No, I'm broke. No, I'm not properly educated. No, I hate yard work. No, I loathe gyms. No, I despise sacrificing life for labor. No, I deplore cars. No, vacations are for suckers. No, I hate you. Keep your sweaters and cigars.

So I listened, hopelessly listened to use their own ammo on them later with this book. A cog whimpers somewhere in Bruno and I see a mother fiddling with its paw. Few lamas and camels and goats sniffed our boots and butts as we passed by. The kids, the kissing kids splashing in the dirt and roaring in shadows were happier than the fattest American kids locked on couches on evenings like this. These little Chadians were reassuring yet heart-shattering to see in action.

If transplanted into my home they would die inside the suffering of the city or inside the spiteful suburbs. If enough suburban supermen that I mentioned a few lines ago scrutinized them inside the world in which only they flew around and executed their superpowers the transplants would pass on by like me; alone, disgusted and afraid. There are just too many damn distractions and frivolous responsibilities getting in the way of real happiness now.

Ding! Goes the dinner bell and Mark and I are off to downtown N'Djamena to the World Away Bar in a flat-black jeep, leaving the old white bus back in Bruno. We rolled ahead from desert to suburbs to city.

Downtown N'Djamena clamored like the jingling jewelry on so many displays on so many sidewalks in so many shopfronts on so many sweating bodies. And outside the hot jeep on the fuming street, I let Mark lead the way. We settled into a wooden booth on the side of the bar with the hardwood seat spiking my tailbone and testing my back.

"Do you have enough room?"

I bumped his feet three inches away, "You're good."

The indoor atmosphere of the World Away Bar teased my memory of summers back home where when you stepped outside it felt like Satan was giving you a big wet hug. The wall of fried air flowing from the kitchen rested over us with the beer and piss shooting upwards from beneath the table. And here it was, intimacy – the intimacy I wanted in the shape of this person named Mark Hubble. Shaving the shade from his face put me on my toes because for some reason, and my vanity does play favorites, I imagined his spotless aesthetics meant for Rayless were really for me.

And I let his cutting cheekbones, mirroring my own, suck me into a trance. The sinister detachment that any decent novelist curates perched itself on my brain's scaffolding and I became incredulous to my being human, not just a body but a brain running a body, and this brain controlled body was being judged by him as me. This projected image of me is really who I am to him: the handsome and perplexing intellectual. But to myself, I'm just a well-played waxwork.

The idea went to pieces when the drinks arrived and our blood started thinning out.

"So, this is your fifth novel?" his surfer's tone in high tide now.

"Yep, I haven't come up with a general plot yet but I've started it as a journal of sorts: about back home and coming here on the plane. I'll see where it takes me when this is over." "Probably *back home*."

"It's doubtful. I can't go home again."

"Are you the main character, like is he based on you?"

"Yeah, it's autobiographical so far. I don't know everything I'll do yet but I'll make it memorable no matter what. It's going to be my first published novel and the most important of our generation. People won't believe it when they finish it. I might not even believe it."

"That sounds pretty unbelievable. Why can't you go home again?"

"Because of the memory of my father and how bad it is there. At least here you can help people and make a difference, all you can do is suffer back there. You can't help people there like you can here."

"Most people have to help themselves before they can help others." He let one knee sleep on my quad. "I'm getting a text from Rayless. The signal is back. Do you have a phone?"

"No, not yet. I knew I wouldn't know anyone here so I didn't bother getting one before I left."

I saw a notification appear on his screen, "What did she send you?"

"Oh, it's the vintage swimsuit she brought with her. She's got really unique tastes. She loves everything vintage. We talked about going swimming soon and she said she'll wear it for me." My mental check-list checked one more item: conceit. The set-ups Rayless used for us men-children were timeless and terrible. I kept our plans for tonight hidden from him. I didn't mind sharing her with Mark, as so he didn't know. Remember the two cakes I mentioned at the beginning of this novel?

Rayless and I appeared passive but were possessive in our snares, unlike Mark. Rayless and I were that exotic flower most pass in the wild without mind, but on a hard-luck day, an unseen butterfly will be snatched up by the alluring and delicate Beelzebub. She would be far more candid with me because she knew I was on her level, and she was. She would morph Mark's protected heart into her own personal plaything only to bring her gavel down to obliterate him.

After getting what she wanted he would be cut loose until a new victim she approved of came along. I was banking, and still am, on the awkward disheveled cynic who also pretends to be fascinated by vintage swimwear.

"When's the big swim date with you two?"

His own mental notification appeared, looking away from the screen up to me again, "Um, this week sometime. We can skip dinner or eat early then leave for the night if you want."

"That sounds good. I know I want this book to be underscored in blood. I just need a plausible excuse to do it. I need an opening I can use."

"Send me a copy."

Busy black patrons bubbled over carbonated amber water, aka Chadian beer. The counterfeit liquor bottle used for my glass had a typo on its face: J&B Bourdon.

"I will." Of course, I couldn't tell him about the part he plays in it.

"In my thirties, I want to give this up for the most part and finally use my teaching degree in America. I got my degree but no one was hiring and networking got so boring that I just decided to leave my parents' home to do this a while back. I've always wanted to help people, even when it wasn't the most practical thing to do in the moment."

"So, what grade would you give this experience."

"Um…this season is definitely a B so far. The last four have been A's. But I want to make this my last season here. I want to leave feeling accomplished. I need to pay off all my debt or I'll never leave my dad's place."

"How is your dad?"

His knee awoke and probed around, hitting the table before he glued them back together.

"He's great. He's still the best person I know." His subtle defense at my slight intrusion made me wonder.

"How great is he?"

"He's just the best person I know."

"Well, I'm sure you've learned more from doing this than living with him. And teaching shitty first world kids would have been a poor substitute for this experience."

"Yeah, but both groups have their value."

"Just not equal value. Ironically we can get on here but I think most Chadians wouldn't handle the first world well. There are too many restrictions, too many distractions, and superficial responsibilities. It's much more meticulous and stressful to have it good, I think."

"Why?"

"Because you're under the delusion that stuff that doesn't matter does."

"I never thought of that."

"That's because you're not a novelist and you didn't come where I'm from. I had tons of freedom back home because I lived in the worst city in North America and arguably the world. Because no one cares about it and it's neglected you can be left alone forever and never be told what to do."

"Kind of like here."

"A little."

The kind sullen waiter took our orders. Mark unfolded one arm across the back of the bench and slouched to one side. "Do you like being a writer?"

"Being a reader and a writer at this stage in this age makes me feel like a hawk scrounging for scraps in a finely preserved wasteland." His angular face molded a wolf's grin.

"I always want to hide inside someone's skull, beside their mind. I want to see and feel everything as they do and bounce it off me. I want to invade and marry minds. It's not from insecurities, envy or voyeurism…I just love people so much."

"Do you like people?"

"I like getting away with being one."

He posed for a toast by covering his smile with his black beer, "Well, I wish you luck in getting it published."

"Thanks, Rabbit." Assuming his new nickname was a heady reference he smiled as he gulped. I cauterized the subject with, "Authors have the deepest personalities because we have the most to report."

One slight nod to my statement and he swerved the talk, "How long has it been since you've had a girlfriend?"

"I've had a string of one night stands for the longest time but I haven't had an official girlfriend in three years."

"How was she?"

"I'll just say there's nothing like dating a girl who's been raped by her dad. There's nothing she won't do and nothing she can't do."

"Jesus..."

"It was a while ago and her memory doesn't bother me anymore."

"What did you do before coming here - besides college and debt?"

"I was a restaurant manager for four years and a bartender for two years before that. I found out early on working in a restaurant that humoring people 24/7 gets old fast. I could do it because I always believe in people too much."

"Don't feel bad. I've been missing the picture since day one. Teachers used to post my I.Q. on the sides of milk cartons." His haughty chuckle fluttered overhead. Somewhere between our exchange the food came and steamed like a micro English moor at midnight: something fried, something baked and something steamed.

We bravely ate our meals muted. I ordered another Bourdon after the hot runny greens were gone. I bypassed the hot brown clump of growth. I sucked and picked my teeth while Mark picked a nostril – not uncommon manners in Chad.

"You want to walk around?"

"We can walk up and down the avenue a little to see if there are any new bars or shops. I haven't just walked around here in almost four months." Two Francs sporting ditch diggers and chauffeurs waited under our glasses. "Watch out for pickpockets. A couple of volunteers already lost their wallets walking around."

Blubbering motorbikes and choking cars zoomed and crawled beside on Avenue De Galle.

"How about this?" *'Liqueur, bière et vin'* was painted on a dusted edifice along our path. Unwashed armpits and fermented grapes greeted us inside the aisles. He settled on a generic 40 oz. of beer while my palate declared 'Yes!' at the crystal bottle of Francis' gin. Yes, back at Bruno the gin sweetened my tongue and kissed my brain over and over again as I drank it under Africa's shattered diamonds smeared across scores of molten acrylics. Slurp, exhale, inhale, repeat.

I waited behind golden sandstone, masking my silhouette behind the rock as I waited twenty yards outside the village in the desert at my dead fire pit. Between the black echo-walk of night and me, I watched Rayless bend forward to slip her panties down inside our open tent spilling with lamplight. When she dimmed the light and stepped into the frozen sand, being guided through the night by moonlight, I knew as her figure approached that love was a museum piece. And it would crumble in my hands if I got them around the glass.

Chapter 5

"Since death is longer than life, life is death's reward. And I think the weight of life and death is blunted, if not lost, because of all the self-made static we're living in now." Nya parked a flat horizontal hand over her brow, looking confused inside the hue of my newly acquired sunglasses. She heaved a polite and feminine sigh, "Do you know how to dance?"

"Here, you can use my glasses."

Sliding them onto her nostrils and fitting them behind her ears I answered her baffling question, "I only dance when I'm listening to music or drinking with friends." Her bulbous black face flashes me behind my beaming black shades.

"No, you should dance to be happy. We're having a birthday party for one of the children and we're all going to dance after we sing for him, even the other volunteers. I want to see you dance and be happy instead of saying all of these bad ideas about life, death, and your country. I think you think too hard so please dance with us. The kids and the women love you even when you're very quiet when no one talks to you."

To be celebratory about anything always felt defiant towards my natural gargoyle-on-a-spire self. True, I had talked to the point of bragging about my hands-on experience of hunting with my sharpshooting father (and butchering our catches) back home, but only because it was seen as a relatable and impressive skill here. To dance on a dime and destroy my poetic image for something as silly as a child's birthday bash was deeply unacceptable. But I'll concede her hearty plea broke a sensual ripple that washed over my dignity. Her plea was more gushing and less devious than Rayless's, whom I hadn't spoken to in four days - since our night in the cold dark desert together.

"Why do they love me?"

"You're always alone and quiet. You're very well mannered. They want to you know what you're writing when you're alone. Most of them are excited to learn how to read when the school is finished. You should have fun with us. We want to see you happy like everyone else. Oh come on, let's dance today. I'll teach you."

Her overbearing candor and oozing elation did finally intimidate me. I had to fold. I couldn't seriously hold anything against her. "Sure, I'll dance."

"Good," she rolled out her O's, "The school should be done in a week and we'll dance then too. Okay?"

"Yes. You can keep the glasses."

"Gustave will thank you later but I will now," she intruded into my face. The intense solar heat was snuffed when her pillowed lips placed a kiss on my cracked mouth. She dotted her gratitude with, "You're very beautiful." And a blossoming grin followed.

"Thank you, you are too."

Rayless had said it, now Nya confirmed it. But it never matters. Beauty ruins more lives than anything else and knowing that always makes me feel like a villain when someone shows me any warmth. I suppose I chalk it up to us being a predatory species and my quiet exclusion from that terrible behavior makes me forever leery of the human herd.

But that's why I have such good luck with people sometimes. I perform as a blank, polite prop so others can imagine devouring me for themselves. Everyone loves the hunky blank mannequin carved from ivory. The male model with detached eyes can be possessed and controlled. He's your doll. And I'm that ugly.

She backed away and turned hut-ward before she could see my real ugliness. The blubber of two topless cream colored jeeps rolled into Bruno twenty feet from the well. Two white trekkers from America jumped from each. Nya swirled to them en route to husband Gustave, "Heeelo!" Khaki shorts and ruddy boots with brown knee-high socks, goofy safari hats resembling amputated octopi atop cheap sunglasses – they shared handshakes with her.

I strolled over to listen and back her up – no matter how weak and childish the delusions of pride and protection are to me. Bruno was growing into my own home now and the thought, connected with the feelings, motivated my work ethic among other newly oiled mechanisms of my character. Their low chatter unclamped itself for my ears every step I took.

I deciphered from the typical face man, "Have there been any by here?" Nya shook them off with coy theatrics; the innocent humility and virginal maneuvers of false ignorance.

The faceman reached into a gross leather-bound wallet and extracted a card to hand over, "Please reach us here if they or the elephants pass through, okay?" She bowed her head to the sand.

A purring stealth-black jeep hiding behind one straw hut dug its way to the two whites. Four militant blacks shouldering AK-47s and holstering .1911s in full military fatigues were briefed. They saluted Nya and the few kids gathering at her calves. Off they chug across the sand to the permanent hills, the immovable mountains and off to where camel urine burns up dead growth in the fairy tale of ancient nature.

"Nya, who were they?" She stepped in to whisper, "Poacher hunters. The white people work for Zakouma Park with the elephants. And the black soldiers are Chadian soldiers the government lends to the parks to help stop the poachers." Sound the first row of bells

The idea was crouched in tall grass, warming-up its shoulders to pounce. I felt my brow crumble to a hard bridge of concentration.

"See, you're upset again." Nya cupped my rotator cuff and mashed the fossilized nerves away. I smiled a lip-full but she held on for a dozen more seconds.

"Do the park rangers or the poacher hunters ever kill the poachers?"

"Sometimes, I know a couple of poachers who were killed. But they don't get paid, and if they do it is not much. It is a big problem with helping them help the elephants."

"It's legal to kill the poachers if you're a poacher hunter?"

"Yes."

"Well, fortunes are never made by hard work."

This alien admittance riled her all over. The warmth she faced me with fizzled. I felt like a pee-on who betrayed his master, "In America, that's the case. But of course, here it's totally different." She calmed any lava-like burst she might possess and coolly retorted, "Fortunes are different for you and me. Not everyone needs money to be wealthy."

Down go the targets on the range. Naked? Eager? Embarrassed? Yes! But I've been those things many, many times before and knew to let her dominate – to save face by avoiding a spilling explanation or take a sissy's exit with a shrug and a smile. After surviving poverty for so long, nothing is embarrassing. I only politely pretended to understand my ignorance.

And what charm she used to leave me: the good-luck-bud departure soldiers in movies give when parting for blood. I yelled something about the dance that week and she only showed one side of her leer over her shoulder. I still have the feeling, the awful villainous pull in me, that whenever I piss someone off I should be paid for the effort. I watched a growing little dust devil dancing outside the village as I walked blindly ahead.

I arrived at four teenage girls huddled at lightning-branched tree giggling at a spare Avid Africa pamphlet. Half heartbroken, half apologetic I asked what was giggle-worthy. Their leader pointed and explained. Her little finger underlined a young, fashionable white know-nothing with a beard. She spoke defiantly and mocked the dope while the teeny-boppers snickered. I imitated them and shook my head at the picture.

Whew! They bought it. The little dusty cyclone fanned off somewhere and I noticed the mothers of Bruno around the well with babies in arms and toddlers at shins. I saw these poor black mothers feeding their children back home, moving along I-696 in sluggish vans and oafish trucks hauling a jumbo-size trailer to some dumpy campsite for a rendezvous with Jet-Puffed Jumbo Puffs, Aunt Tickles' Graham Goodies and Harry's Hearty Hershey. Oh, and don't forget the light beers in the dwarf fridge. I saw them transplanted into the high life of American poverty. Where's the fucking giant? Where's the tent? Where's the stupid dinner bell or work whistle? I needed to nap.

*****

I retired from the rest of the afternoon by digging up fertile earth with my black and grey sneakers (what an appropriate name for my footwear) while the sun branded me clay red. All hundred plus villagers and twenty-odd volunteers massed at the well – all but me still kicking around in outer orbit. Lethargy won and I just observed to see if any quality commotion would show for me to leave my haze of sun and sand. Fifty or so migrated to one lone diaper hut with a blond wig of straw crowning the heap. I stepped from sand to soil. Mark hissed at me from inside the tent as I passed.

"What do you want? I thought you would be with the others. Are you stealing my style?"

His crunched frame sat wrapped and curled inside. "Come in. I want to talk." I stepped in and crouched inside beside my buddy stinking of wet body odor and warm milorganite.

"What's up?"

A boyish sigh prefaced his rant, "It's about Rayless. She uh…she spent some time with you."

"…"

His clumsy conviction levied any stress about making convincing lies - this guy will buy anything.

"We talked for a bit in the desert a few nights ago. I couldn't sleep and she couldn't either so we started a fire and caught up."

"I just want to know your opinion of her. Like, what do you think?"

"She's really great." How I loved and loathed normal 'guy' speak: love getting away with it but loathe my demotion of dignity. "I mean, she's really smart and nice…sexy too. Go for it."

He remained slumped wearing a confused mask of trauma. With my sly coaching and limp championing, I knew what insecure, predatory coaches feel when yelling their loud, ugly and un-motivational words at fat, helpless and retarded kids at fat, helpless and retarded camps. Or during the fat, helpless and retarded sports games of their fat, helpless and retarded parents' choice for that entire fat, helpless and retarded summer. He was now fat, helpless and retarded and I at once saw how those creeping ghouls stay employed all summer.

"Go for her." More dim silence on the high towers end.

As a wooden statue coming to life, he cracked his appendages before declaring his impotent ambitions, "I just think she's really great and I'm going to tell her." He went to explain his frivolous and childish attractions; this music reference hinted, that approved TV show joke and the internet memes shared over an awkward night of cell phones, shy chuckles, anemic beers and watery whiskeys.

"So you're made for each other!" I do love my cynical enthusiasm.

"I just hope she's into me too. You think she likes me, right?"

"Mark, how the hell can you be so tender and unsure? You have everything going for you. You're the king here and she's goddamn Anna Karenina. Who else is she going to see?"

"You."

Quick lie, like a champion fighter eluding the hook fired at his chin to save his ass, "Give me a break. She likes talking to me because I'm a writer and I know women so well. But she doesn't love."

Correction – she did love me, but not in the way I wanted her to. I haven't divulged the hellish night Rayless and I spent in the icy desert with you, silent reader, or with him (yet). Nope, that comes as my crimson cherry of delight pinched atop this story.

"She likes you...uh, I can tell." For the past week his absence of enthusiasm or affection left me indifferent to his welfare, and knowing that no one could love Rayless and vice versa, I encouraged his pursuit in the dull, drab, humdrum, water-cooler speak all one-dimensional baboons engage in. "Man, just do it. She's great. What have you got to lose?"

All convincing, all fake. His neck uncurling like an albino snake from a hemp basket, "Yeah?"

"Yeah." He was so damn lovable. The awkward impasse romance leaves friends at arrived so I swerved the talk, "Do you know what's going on in that hut out there?"

"No, why? Does it look bad?"

I scrunched my brows and shook my head in a tell-me gesture.

"I ask because the reason people came here to start their new village was that famine wiped most of them out in Mao. They came here five years ago and have needed help since. They lived on the outskirts of Mao," he rubbed his lanky white paws over dead sockets to buffer his interest in telling it again, "But the only thing going against us here is the weather and the money. We don't need mother nature slapping us again this season."

"It has been a harsh summer so far."

"All the vegetation the women are growing is anemic and half dead, the goats and other animals aren't eating as much and most of the men who have jobs in town had their hours slashed because of the economy."

I had no input, not after his anxiety over a girl like Rayless. Men like Mark Hubble, if not mothered by other men or women, will forever run from themselves long before they can face themselves. I was done dealing with his feeble drama and his cheap spicy cologne tugging my nose hairs.

I leaped from the vinyl. It was a relief to get a human, all too human, scent in my nostrils again at the rioting hut. Mingled mumbles escalated in the epicenter of the mob. The elderly, missing their teeth and draped in old world colors, crossed themselves in the corny theatrical solitude one demands when making a scene with prayer in public. Nya narrowly nicked her way beside me and I crushed her elbow with my grip, "What's happening?"

She clamped down on my hand and moved me with her, "Come with me. We'll find a doctor." She shouldered her way to the tent with me at her hip. I picked up her preachy frequency inside the human static, "We have a doctor in Bruno now and it's a blessing. Some say it's a gift and a sign. This is what happens when everyone rushes towards a miracle."

Nya hissed at the opening, "How is he? Is the doctor still here?"

The doctor emerged behind knelt bodies as we peeked inside the hushed tent, "Yes, I'm here." The grunt he made when his creaky knees strained to rise was that of a helpless dad wrestling with a kidney stone knifing his innards. Every dumb doctor pun ran through me but I had to be quiet. My presence riveted me because they knew nothing about me and ignored my being one foot away. I was a tag-along spectator with no role, no purpose or promise of ability.

Nya held her breaths under the surface, not letting them boil to hysterical heaves, while Dr. Suburban Santa Claus stood inside the musky padding of his long salted beard. I would be so ashamed to be as fat and greasy as him in this situation though Nya, I'm sure, let those gross observations slide to the back of her short mind. His solid gut was tucked under a pink polo shirt and resembled a meteor wrapped inside cotton candy.

I got behind Nya because he smelled of bacon, dirty hair and old books. Huffing while adjusting his strangling belt he walked a hippo's pace beside Nya from the hut. For every one person who sidestepped Nya four moved for him. Arriving at the neighboring igloo I froze inside the opening. An ancient black witch huddled over a small fire pit centered below the roof's little round opening. She kindled a smoking mess of incense, insensitive to the toddler wheezing tiny breaths from his failing chest.

The witch hummed a monotonous mantra while Nya knelt to the child and the doc positioned himself like a retiring whale on a beach. From somewhere, maybe from under his galactic gut, he removed a medical bag and extracted a rubber loop, a pocket square of gauze, a Q tip and one packaged syringe. In goes the needle, out goes the blood. This kid, and how proud I am of him, didn't (or couldn't) react with a wince or a scream. His asthmatic breath was somehow comforting to me.

"Okay, okay...good." His cautious first-world tone did nothing to sooth the kid. Nya helped the hammy hematologist to his feet, "We'll see what the test says in fifteen minutes. I won't say it looks good, we just have to see. If he's positive, he is treatable but everyone in the village will need to be tested immediately."

She acknowledged with a somber and frantic nod. Doctor Hindenburg strained for take-off but eventually floated back to home base.

"Nya..." She rubbed her hand across the bulging naval of the boy then looked when I called her again. She stood staring down at him, then bolted from the tent with me in hand again. Through the curious begging crowd, we ran to a group of emptied huts on the precipice of the village. Her eyes pooling she gargled out some words, "This can't happen here. If he is infected, then more could be - we would have to test and treat them. There is only one doctor here and we need tests, treatment and, and…"

"Quarantine."

"What does that mean?"

"Keep the infected away like you do sick animals from the healthy ones."

"Yes…"

Already lost behind a hurtle of horror stretching around the globe several times, she pierced the empty space beside my right shoulder with the most disturbed gaze I'd ever seen. Only later on did I see that watching-of-invisible-horrors again and again.

She gently flung her arms around my neck and glued her cheek to my chest. I love real love. Using traditional corniness everyone understands, I lifted my lungs high and hard for her to feel secure and nestled. And it worked (I think, I hope). Her hot body rested as a line of kids and a few fathers scampered to the end of Bruno for us.

Cheers and jeers flanked the huts and they looked back. Nya stayed resting. The parade parted and showed one lone bull elephant leisurely swaying among the people. Brown as the baby in the school but five times its size, the white sabers of ivory curled to the black floor of Bruno on either side of his dusty trunk. I suddenly saw this animal tapping Nya to demand its baby back. What a cartoonish mind I have.

"Nya, look…" Queue the gasp of one woman in sight of a cute object. Her heat dashed with the rest of her and left me all ice. French was exchanged between her and the kids with the creature. As I walked over I admired her selflessness at hiding her rotting conscience from the kids. At close range, I smirked up to its wrinkled jet-black marble eyes draped in spider-leg lashes.

Nya slipped her light, hard hand into mine and took me off, out of earshot from the phonic kids, "Can you please dial this number? We can't keep two elephants here. That one is too big for the children to play with." The white card was already damp and creased from hiding between her breasts.

"Let me see it…"

The header read Graham 'Birdy' Grape - underpinned by a phone number, fax number, and email. "I don't have a phone now. I really don't have anything. But I'll get one of my friends to dial it. What do you want to do?"

"Give him to the park in Zakouma. We cannot keep him here. The baby – fine, but no adults. It's too much now."

My thin nylon shorts had no pockets so I planted the card into my left sock – an old hometown trick for carrying valuables. Lisa Little's little limbs jittered with fright with me tucking my body beside her in her side of the tent. She and Rayless' toiletries were dumped around their sheeted floor. I now saw how they junked themselves to face the world every afternoon.

A closed box of tampons sat beside a vintage makeup bag leaking accessories. A low wall of rumpled clothes lay along six pairs of shoes. Lisa lay silently sleeping face down on her blow up mattress. I nudged her naked shoulder until she moaned awake.

"I need to use your phone to call someone for Nya about the elephant."

She groaned an 'okay' and unlocked her phone for me, "Just leave it there when you're done."

The heavy electronic blurb sounded twice, "Hello?"

"Hi, Bridy Grape? I'm calling from Bruno village." I'll be a transparent tattle tale and tell you I was hurried along by a low bubbling fear in my guts as I informed him of the new elephant at Bruno. Naturally, I forgot about the baby, but we worked out a pick-up order for one African bull elephant.

"Thank you again. The poachers around here will do anything to kill a bull with this much ivory. We just want to keep him and the village out of harm's way. Thank you."

The pickup was scheduled for eight A.M. tomorrow. Birdy assured me of the beast's welfare in Zakouma Park. He warned outright, "Do not sell yourself to poachers, because they'll pay you, but the problems that follow will not be worth it. You'll have them and the government after you. You're doing the right thing by lending yourself to us."

"I understand. Thank you. I'll see you at eight tomorrow morning."

The devilish ace snoring in my sleeve would fall to my aid quicker than anticipated and my own plot, decorated with delicious collusion, would take form fast. "Here you go Lisa."

"Mhmmm"

"Sorry – thanks." Signaling for rescue under a pink and white sock was an American fifty dollar bill. I stepped on it, tied my shoes and pocketed it.

"What's going on out there?"

"Not much: just new news, but same as always." The limp blimp collided with me on our way to Nya. I asked how the boy was.

"I want to tell Nya first." Half the crowd was with the bull and the others were still at the hut; mostly women and a few serious men. The rotted witch had disappeared. On my knees beside Nya and Dr. Pepper, he groaned a number: A3/02. Attached was the tonal belch of, "I hope it's not that one. It was found last year in West Africa and its spreading fast. We'll have to take him into N'Djamena for testing and treatment, but he does have it." She kneaded one of the child's soles with one of her free hands. Colonel Sanders clucked solutions out as the fatal silence fried him, "I'll contact WHO to send volunteers for us. They can bring all the tests we need. The UN just opened a committee to deal with this. We will stop it. Medical assistance is constantly being given to us by the health organization."

All of his ballooning encouragement couldn't nudge Nya. "I'll get on the phone now." The back splitting and joint cracking of his body combined with the desperate grunt of uncertainty when he struggled to his feet nearly bombed my diaphragm. But enough. I'm not running fat cells from my pen's head but hot blood, remember? Outside, hearing his startled voice announce in cowering desperation he had, "some bad news, Jerry. I need a number." I thought of him realizing he was speaking to a spare Twinkie in his pocket and not his phone. What a sweet, scrumptious mistake that would be. My cartoonish brain pops once more!

I hope so far, at some point, drops of spit have graced my words on your copy of this book from laughter. If you can't see the dried mist of saliva pattering's don't keep looking for them. Let them petrify inside these pages. Let them stay as hallmarks of your good nature. We need little traces of ourselves sprinkled over our experiences so fossils and momentous live up to their potential.

I used to leave more intimate and less ambitious traces of myself on the world. I knew I was never worth knowing or following, not then. When I walked down corroded suburban streets back home, especially during winter, I knew when I was gone the swooning bb of spit splashing onto the ice-laminated cement would be evidence of some kind of my invisible life. It would only briefly litter this little planet with no credit coming my way as I strolled under the dome of arctic glitter and cosmic streaks. No credit was ever given to me but I knew my influence, on some level, had been planted like dirty evidence. An ongoing investigation will begin, no doubt, after the first printing of this book.

Back in the hut, I lassoed Nya with a tragic truth to remove her from her own melancholic rumination over the boy. I rolled out a heavy and slight declaration, "It's hard for men to find love. No one loves men for being men. If we don't find people to love us, if we don't try, no one will ever come. This is a lifetime talking." She switched from stroking the child's foot to rubbing his chest.

She was really rubbing out her fears on him when she hissed a nose-full of thought. "The world is hard, not soft. Look at this boy…"

"At least he has a woman rubbing him. No one will ever rub me, at least not the right way."

"How come you think like this?"

"Because my home was broken. Do you know how that felt? My city, my home, my family, my schools and me. My father used to make me hunt and butcher animals. He would insult me, humiliate me, and cuss at me for being a child. Do you know how that felt? I was born in life's anus. I was cut off from any chance of a decent life before I could speak. I've been in exile my whole life. Please tell me how I can forget these things to experience better things? I really think if there's someone who could change my mind about the world it's you."

Her hand quit working on the boy. She repositioned her sandy black feet on the dirt floor. "You overcome bad memories by making good memories."

My larynx nearly exploded. She was so damn right, so fucking correct in the most honest and foolish way! I knew I could never find good things to pursue and I'll be forever damned if good things ever find me. For the first time in Africa, I almost cried in the spot where I stood. I can't ever fully illuminate that dungeon door to my past for anyone. When I slip up and try it always leads to thoughts of suicide. Suicide is the only recourse for someone as deluded and useless as me.

What's an unlovable person to do besides kiss this flash in the pan we call a life goodbye? I've known my whole life suicide is the only way out for me. I'm cursed knowing life will never be kind enough to just kill me off quickly. Life is never kind, only you can be kind to yourself. Fuck it all!

The strained blob wobbled back inside. Cough, sniff, and fart: "Nya, we have to take him into N'Djamena first. To see what kind it is, what type of strain and how advanced it is. WHO will send a team out here to investigate, but I want to take a sample of his blood for myself. My friend Jerry is a doctor volunteering in town and he'll give me his opinion and will look after him. I'll get everything ready now." He plunged the blood from the boy's little forearm. Gustave and his male pals assisted with the boy while Nya looked on.

I stayed in the hut. The outside noise was divided between the elephants' commotion and the crowd preparing to transfer the boy. Eventually all disappeared while night invaded Bruno, and naturally, no one looked for me. No one found me. Goddamn me. Back in the tent (I can't say 'our' tent because it would hurt too much) I wrote a little quick gush of doomed prose. I want to leave this crude and unedited, really unfinished, sample of myself from that night – that oh so important night that now stands as the turning tide of my tale.

It was when I became an exclamation mark. It was the night the light bulb flicked atop my scalp and burst with hysterical shock. It was when I got the horrid idea of spreading blood on my gears. Here are my dumb, typical lines from that expletive night:

'We have no real jobs or tasks to complete. Friends come and go on and offline. I sometimes cry tears of dumb bravado when I think of the work (my writing) I did alone with all the others like me lost across America dying in youth from failures of the new human heart. All of my friends are already gone. But I slipped sorrow's noose with this – coming home to Africa to roost. I don't even want to see the mess that shows with my believing I'll be a published author with *this* book.

To all the friends I almost kept and to the ones I cut out of my life for whatever abusive reason – I'm sorry! I'm so goddamn sorry! I still love you and it's my fault! I watch outside this hut. Van Gough never saw what I'm seeing now. I miss everyone because memories are all I can love.'

And on that tired note of timeless pain and stupid young agony that no one has time to consider anymore, I leave before I return. See you on the next page!

Chapter 6

The end of my languishing night in the stale hut came when I started watching sunbeams laser over the meridian of mountains. A rogue piece of my self was already starting the virgin day by running me down. And then a snake, a sneaky little scaly slinky appeared as a fanged spine inching on the earth. Its approach scooted me a few feet back. Before it inspected the fire pit a toddler boy walked in and snapped it back by its tail and left like it was business as usual.

Curiosity compelled me to slip out and gaze from a low crouch at the three boys and one single grandma now handling the snake by straightening its coil like a string. She held it down as she told one boy to lop its heart-shaped head from its squirming body. Off rolls the head, mouth ajar in a silent scream, as she proceeds to skin its still wiggling body with a shoddy potato knife. Somewhere in my past, I saw my father grunting orders and barking demands for me to clip off the arms and legs of the turtles we caught on a rented boat in a filthy great lake. The silent little tanks of green and brown writhed as I filleted off their meat to stumps. And then I hunkered down before he slapped me to slice the heads off, chucking the little appendages in the water. Turtle soup anyone?

Snake soup was a timely delicacy the elders of Bruno concocted for the kids on certain mornings. I could have ingratiated myself by showing them my fellow Neolithic knowledge by butchering the snake to impress them but those pesky flashbacks prevented me from imitating the kid I once was. I would never use those skills again. All the popularity and fame in the world would never be incentive enough to butcher anything again.

After she finished boiling the creature in a black cauldron over a smoky fire I decided to trade my morning misery for some fresh interaction. I felt daring enough to test out new people in Bruno because only at night or in the early morning am I drained enough to communicate with no edge. Having coffee or cocktails is most appropriate for me to speak.

So when Nya intercepted me like a punted football en route to the snake eaters I had to wonder why she was village headmaster to all the children. Was she too retarded to work? Is husband Gustave letting her fulfill the thwarted female ambitions her parents and grandparents failed to accomplish in their times? On arriving at the four killers Nya snagged my bicep shoved a concerned smile in my face.

"Please, let me make you breakfast instead. I want to try to make you happy finally."

Ah! She knew me well enough by now to know how hurt I'd be to see them serve their breakfast. She also didn't want to embarrass her fellow villagers in my eyes. I was touched by her worry, but more annoyed with her slyness.

"Nya, I have to ask since you seem to be like a godmother to all of the children here. Do you have kids?"

"No, I cannot have children."

I should have felt repentant for my slight offense, but I knew that no kids from her meant more kids for her. She will always be netting and replacing children to make up for her own injury, so I wasn't too sorry.

"I'm sorry."

"My husband said he liked it when I told him." Her bulbous cheeks aimed a shy smile at my sneakers - half embarrassed, half amused.

"I envy him sometimes. Where is Gustave? Sometimes he works with us for a while and then he's gone."

"Oh, he has a job in town. He drives a cab for people."

Despite all of my run-ins with cabbies back home stealing the frequency on police bands and jabbering my fucking head off with talks of their wasted lives that have landed them hauling drunks and dopes around a deathly city, I still congratulated her on his having a job. This is the formula for any working people: Work = God, Leisure = Satan. *'He shovels hippo shit off the lawns of drug lords in the nice part of town? You must be very proud.'*

Letting the lovable heathens eat their snake shit I allowed Nya to beguile me away. "Do you want to travel abroad too, like me? It must be embarrassing showing how Chad and Bruno are over and over again to vacationers."

She palmed my wrist, "Oh no! It is true; I will travel, unlike my parents and grandparents. Few men have done it and no women here have yet. I would be the first. Other women here want to also, but it is so expensive to travel and to get educated."

"Oh, believe me, I know."

"How did you get here?"

"I saved up a lot of money." Which is the truth but the savings was allowed because of my dying grandmother's cancerous brain being too clogged with tumors to remember if she had $50 in her purse yesterday or $5. And chemotherapy does wonders for thieves. I casually went on about the honorable job I cherished at the gas station, affording me this luxurious ease into which I stepped into Chad to be a better, more complete animal. She took what I gave at face value and opened up with more shocking, yet natural, truths about the history of rural people sprinkled over rural Chad.

We paused under thinly veined trees without growth, "See, the older women here, like the grandmothers and great grandmothers – that is what you call them *back home?*"

"Yes."

"Well, the way they got married and had children is much different than in America. You see, I understand other cultures would not be accepting or understanding of my culture. Now, I'm not saying I will never leave, but I will have to take that understanding with me." How I cherished her loquacious French accent.

"Are there any specific things you keep guard of that you want to share with me?"

"Yes."

Priming herself she clapped both hands once then relieved her lungs of fear, "Those women you see playing with the children, not me, but the older ones. All of their children came from rape. And most of their husbands kidnapped them and raped them so that afterward they were forced to marry."

"And how do they get on with that?" (Though I already knew).

"They are happy women. They love their kids and their husbands. It was explained to them as little girls that that is what happens for a girl to become a woman."

"I understand." And I did. Of course, there was no internet search for verification of the women's happiness, but sometimes you don't need it. They didn't come from the internet. They came from a more expansive and unbelievable world.

"Of course it's no longer the tradition. Our generation stopped that here." Ah, but how many generations said that of their shameful past. Look real hard all over the sketchier parts of the globe and you'll see as much regression and progression.

"I hope so. It's nice to have moral ambitions."

"I treat my ambitions like they are my own children, the ones I wish I could have. Your ambition is writing I see you're strict with it every day. Have you met anyone who has read your books?"

"Ha! I'm not published yet, and I don't think I ever will be."

"Why?"

"The stuff I write, really all literature, has terminal cancer. It won't die though. From now on it will be held up by a tiny batch of cultish elitists. There's no more money or interest left in literature to publish someone like me. No one in publishing takes real risks anymore. I could put my book on the internet but it would be just as wasteful as burning it or tucking it away until my death. Reading is how people were entertained and educated before the internet and everything else. I think I'm playing a kid's game, and after I finish the book I'm writing here I'm ready to stop and grow up. I don't want to be a lonely person forever. I just want to lie to myself well enough with the help of bad friends, quick lovers and borrowed money to at least pretend I lived a full life."

Some of my heady ideas were lost on her but I couldn't explain myself again. She got the general whiff of my disgruntled diatribe.

"Are you sad to stop writing?"

Of course, I had to fake the serious, calm and somewhat stoic head shake and follow with a quick and heavy, "No." 'Me give up the only thing I'm good at, the only thing I can do? Kamikaze the only thing that ever validated my existence? Stop being an improperly educated, broke and dreamy dope? Me having to kiss my own ass goodbye? So much for destiny, legacy and a clown's birthright. No, I'm not upset. It's just one less distraction. Someone said all art is distraction. I like that. I'll let my readers (hopefully) judge this book on that criterion…this stupid old distracting medium of longwinded trash. I want to jump and run in the sun instead of tap these dumb lines on a goddamn keyboard from 1991.' But she accepted my 'no' with graceful finality and didn't want to know more (what a surprise!)

As the blue haze of dawn mystified the camp into a wonderland, a small dust plume grew far away in the desert at the secret spot where you can access hell directly. But as it widened, a dump truck showed itself across the sand, coming from the mountains. As the speed of sound caught up with us, delayed by seconds until it was at Bruno, I remembered with a snarled spine the morning garbage trucks and languid lawn machines being driven up my street by dirty dumbasses. I was hoping this excursion would jumble up the dumb date already. This was a day from the outset that needed a jackhammer's makeover.

But to finish my note about literature being forever dimmed by a sun that doesn't actually rise twice, I know Shakespeare would be better off bussing tables today. That, of course, is just wise speculation. Let us not get swept away by the tide of modern failings. I was already considering being a door greeter at the World Away Bar but I don't speak French or Arabic. I'm already left so far behind like every other wasteful child today that it feels implausible to catch up in any real capacity.

Since I loathe formal education and the racket of college I never bought losing investments backed by mob mentality or majority rule. Hocus pocus focus groups and the like can march on by without a word from me or my sponsor (if I had one to speak for me). But fuck it all! I don't want to talk about boring antique bastards that couldn't hack it in today's world. I want to talk about Nya and Rayless and Lisa. I want to preach about the translucent lines of irony and fate hovering over their lovely bodies and lives, those other-dimensional lines looping and knotting, lassoing if you will, their actions.

But this newly inspired burst of ideas seems too far-reaching, even for me, so I just have to give you more of the story and less philosophy. A good book is a blend of both. Roar, burp, and stutter: the dump truck parked outside the carved wooden archway that declared this village as 'Bruno Village'. Hassan and Gustave hailed the four black army troops and four white park rangers ahead to the school where they put the daddy bull. Nya and a few other mothers held the baby back as the groggy elder limped up a metal ramp to its newly decided home.

A fat brick of bills was handed over to Gustave. Money for animals? Money for money? Anything new? The troops slapped his shoulders in passing as Gustave counted his new fortune. In the end, I couldn't decipher the sounds of the grinding truck from the grunting bull. They both were ushered to another location I would never see. As the men drove the beast off into the desert, Lisa and Rayless returned on a dirt bike. Fart, break, park: they returned the refurbished bike to dummy Hassan.

After a flirtatious exchange with him, they approached me about the news.

"Let me see...some kid might die from some illness in town and they just took an elephant away for some zoo someplace."

"Yeah, we got a text in town from Mark about the kid. Where is he - Mark? How did he know about the kid? I haven't seen him in a ...in at least two days and he wasn't,"

"He just texted me."

"Well text him to find out where he is."

"How's your writing coming along? Got a publisher for it yet?"

"It's going good. But don't talk about it. I don't want to talk about it."

Rayless just petted my arm and moved on, like everyone else. Okay, where is that fucking overgrown moron? Is he here? Nope, that's more kids chasing lamas and camels. Is he there? No. Those are adult children crowding dueling cocks. In all of this shit hole, where is my only real friend? The doctor came rolling back in a sanded jeep. A polyester pouch in one paw and a ream of white papers in another, he huffed and seriously informed me of the kid.

He said something about WHO sending a few people here, something about us going into town for testing and what to do in case of infection with this new strain of AIDS. Super AIDS he called it, "Oh, I won't leave your sight. I love science and I'm curious to what happens." Cryptically bemused by my enthusiasm he moved on to Gustave, Nya and down the totem. Oh, where are you headed my dear bastard? Let me follow, please sir. Going to plunge more blood from the children's doll arms I followed him and the rest of the gatekeepers of Bruno around to the kids and their babyish beds, perhaps soon becoming their death?

Every child's arm gave a little red tube of possible peril. Death is so sad, but life is sadder still. Us adults had to make mock-smiles and faux encouragement to stymie any honest panic these little ones could have about becoming unborn. The summer had long frisked the trees of their cover and spending all this time outside made me feel like Dracula baking in the sun.

The goddamn doctor in his galaxy-bottom jeans having Jupiter and Saturn squeezed into Levi's - he couldn't maneuver his galactic ass away from the poor victims standing by. He just let it rotate around the sons. He fit that black polyester bag with at least thirty needles total. Later on, after he had visited so many children he asked himself, "Was it twenty-nine or thirty? It was thirty."

Of course, he would have butter fingers with something so important. My incriminating judgments prove correct again.

After a gross hospital visit in town the next day, I and every other adult tested negative for A3/02, except for fifteen children. Enter a half dozen WHO volunteers; three from England and three from Iceland. In my last two weeks there Bruno had become a stranger. The air of promise and potential with the village's future went to hell. Even Nya was silent and grim when she tended to the kids.

We workers labored in silence. When we worked on the school it felt like I was doing construction work at a funeral. During this brief phase, Mark divided his busy, busy time between the school, nights in town with Rayless and chatting my ears off with shot after shot at the WAB. I saw beyond the praise of his sacred cow of a father back home. Mark showed just how limited his ambitions were. I pinned it to him still being emotionally underneath his father's oppressive barefoot still dirty from the backyard garden and wet from the dainty sprinkler his sad decoy-wife placed by his sports decorations. His feeble and clumsy passes at me died with the weightless dust inside the WAB drying my eyes to tears.

His transparent hunger for a mutual male romance caused a warm enveloping sadness to cement my insides, below all the cool dry mortar flaking off my skin. He couldn't just accept that side of himself that itched to inch closer and closer to me. His self-thwarting blunders streaked for a few nights at the WAB but were dead by the time we retired to the tent - both of us being too drunk to do anything but blackout.

The WHO people in Bruno wrangled us into groups of four and for three days told us all about how to live with plague among us.

"You make love to live, not live to make love," was my favorite catchphrase from those healthy blonde marshmallows.

Lisa sought me out after one of their well-intended lectures and found me grimacing at an apple-cheeked hog spinning over a late night fire.

She stepped into my side embrace and I shattered her enthusiasm with my horrid disposition, "People who love can't fuck. We all know people who can fuck and don't care about love. Just let love fuck the life out of you, not vice versa."

The squish of her sandals was all I heard. The mutual heat, her little bulb of a body, shut off when she flicked herself away.

How did the children get infected? The armchair geniuses couldn't tell us. Their best theory until all the tests came back consisted of possible child rape. Progress on the school was stonewalled until next week when the children would be released from the hospital with medicines and instructions on how to live the remainder of their short lives.

We didn't separate or quarantine them. Let them have fun, let them live – let us be careful. The funding for the children's treatments was arranged by WHO and by the next week, our revived routines instilled a false normalcy back into the village.

Eventually when the tests were fully completed the six volunteers from WHO along with Dr. Pepper informed us the children only had two years and that anyone infected with this super strain had roughly the same prognosis, despite science's best efforts. I remember thinking 'isn't it time life finally had a conscience?'

Oh well, the kids played in the sun with the other kids and continued to do all the short-term things all kids do. In the second week WHO finally revealed the culprit: four of the parents had been unknowing carriers and had unknowingly passed it onto their children. But I don't want to sadden you anymore, silent reader. There's no point holding back my adventure any longer. I'll move onto the good news that shot me out of Bruno: another bull had lucklessly strolled into the village that week. Gustave called about the terrorist's rates, to see if he would pay more than the park rangers. Who can't use more money? This damn village needs money to live. We all do.

I didn't hear their whole exchange on the phone but somehow I came up during their talk. The terrorist's name turned out to be Ali. And this novel is for him. Ali, thank you for giving me the adventure and the material I needed to pen this masterpiece.

Chapter 7

A deal was struck with this man Ali over the elephant just prior to the last mortared stone being placed in the school to dry. I owe him not the heart and brain of my novel, but the blood and guts of its anatomy. Without him bringing the offer of adventure into my hallow life, your life wouldn't be forever changed by my book, silent reader. I found out quickly that Ali's life was better than fiction. So, as a writer looking for his best-selling idea, how could I not jump at writing the ultimate story about riding life's trail with elephant poachers?

Like so many dead-end job interviews or first days on the job where I bailed like a righteous coward, I bailed on Bruno the day the school was complete. Only this time it was over a terrorist's offer and a promise of the overdue recognition of my genius. We formally met that night, when we all celebrated the future. Ali and his gang endorsed Bruno with their protective company and gifted the adults with party supplies. Their horses stood parked in the outer dark, far outside the light of countless dancing bonfires.

When the party reached its orgasmic pitch Gustave motioned for me to come join him and Ali. "Come here!" He waved one free arm, the one without a bottle, at me to fly over.

On arrival, he introduced me, "This is the strong, serious man." I stood blankly at my drunken induction. Let people think anything of me, only I know better. "He is one of the hardest workers here."

Ali grinned with warm suspicion at me, "I heard you know how to hunt and use a gun very well. Have you killed anything here?"

"No, only back home."

"Can you steal and pickpocket?"

"Somewhat."

Gustave handed the bottle to me, "We can speak freely and ask questions freely, we're all friends here." Ali's one white tooth sparkled particles of fire light at me like a blue star studied closely in the night. It popped at me.

"And I'd like to know what you plan on doing when you're done in Bruno? Do you want to go back home?"

"No, I don't."

"I didn't think so, not given where you're from. Can we talk about your future, if you don't mind?"

"I don't mind, let's talk about it."

"I see a strong young man in you – not like the men you came here with. I've heard some things about you that I like, and since I'm a partner with the village now I'm looking for men to join me and my team. When you're done working here I can pay you to work for me and my men if you'd like?"

See, being from the land of capitalism, where money makes men – not the reverse, I immediately saw Ali as a breakfast sausage tycoon gracing a small flat town in the deep Midwest trying to swoon the governor to allow him to prop his shitty factory just outside the corn-fed capital. Breakfast sausage or ivory, it was all blood and business.

"Killing elephants?"

"Not at first." Tambourines and screaming drums formed a dull streamline of downbeats and encased us.

"What at first?"

"Let's enjoy the party first we'll talk after." I nodded while he stepped away from us. Gustave patted my shoulder for us to move elsewhere. I felt the familiar throb of giving up so now Bruno meant shit.

The women danced in unbounded circles. My rigid sensitivities were keeping me still before they smiled and pantomimed, asking me to join. I started imitating their moves to the fanfare of the viewers on the sideline. I even snatched a Tonga and showed off for a few minutes. For that quick burst, pure jubilation orbited me.

African tobacco hung everywhere, veining the night. I sifted through its weight to find lonely old Mark baited by a dead tree in the dark, the hysteria behind quieting. Looking up at his thoughts in the low branches he flashed his face down when I jabbed his left bicep.

"Hey Rabbit. Are you lonesome tonight?"

"Yeah, a little. What about you?"

"I'm leaving after tonight."

"My mother died three days ago. I got a letter from back home." He obviously didn't hear me.

"Are you coming back here?!"

"Yeah, eventually…" Though I didn't know it then, this proved to be the bridge for ending I was looking for when this story was over. I'm telling everybody, it's the little forgetful things that turn into lifesavers when you really need one.

"Where can I write to you?" I took down his email, phone number and home address in Indiana. I trotted homeward, away from Mark. Rayless was in town with strangers and that knowledge, of her getting revenge on Mark for me so I didn't have to do it myself, made me lust for her all over again.

Ali stood on patches of rippled gold at his own fire pit. Four of his men shuffled a bottle around with cigars stuck between their fingers.

After I stepped over to him I shook his tight rusted hand, "You know me, Al."

"Yes." "Please tell me why you are offering me to join your group? And what is really in it for me?"

I felt the connection his four horsemen had with him resembled what the sinister web is to a devilish spider. He was the spider and they were the webbing. They kept drinking and chattering over their fire with a keen air about them. When Ali cradled my shoulders and walked me away from the fire for a one on one, I saw two men eye us - prepping for the web to be shaken.

He rolled out his speech with a thick choppy accent, "Well…you see you'll be hired by me to work for me and my men. We're not a gang. What we do is supply a demand. People in China and India demand ivory, so we help create the supply. Now, everyone thinks what we do is immoral or against nature. But no one can kill all the elephants off.

There's always going to be people who take care of them and keep them alive. Nobody needs this many fat, ugly beasts fouling our beautiful planet anyway. Really, we're making room in Africa for the people to expand beyond these big, mean and unpredictable creatures. They have no more places in the modern world. People don't need elephants, elephants need people. It's merely unsustainable to have them around in large numbers. So, we help get the trash out of the way for people who will buy it for a fortune. You will get three to five percent of what we take in. An ounce of ivory is worth over one thousand American dollars. When I got into this business four years ago I was a prince with no kingdom and now I'm a king with an empire. I have three villas in southern Africa – all on the ocean. But I'm not soft. I got addicted to hard labor and hunting very young, long before the military. And I taught myself everything in life."

"...Me too."

"When the internet came to Egypt I taught myself how to speak English. Now I hire a language coach for my free time. Many people in the business know how efficient I am. My name carries a lot of weight now. And the business people want to do with me is increasing quickly. I have enough money and resources to stay ahead of the troops and poacher-hunters for years."

That displaced tongue was so damn charming, especially when it came through his hard springy beard.

"But what do you want from me?"

"No one would suspect a young white American man. The authorities look for citizens, not tourists. We're leaving for Mao, up north, tomorrow. Tell me if you are willing to work for us. And before you assume anything about me and my men, I am not a nationalist and do not run a terrorist group. I do not fund dogshit like Al-Shabab, The Lord's Resistance Army or Janjaweed. Ivory is Africa's most profitable export. It's all business for me, nothing more. Well, business and pleasure."

From the shadows, his lone white tooth glittered around his tinted teeth.

I shook his hand, "it's my pleasure to do business together." His lips pouted dramatically and he nodded, "we'll take you into N'Djamena in the morning to test you out."

Like blindly submitting my phony resume on a whim to any place that would have me back home I agreed to a daft deal. Somehow he knew I didn't have a phone and gave me a blank one to use for business.

"Here, I'll call you tomorrow morning at eight. I'll have one of the villagers drive you to town to meet me at the hotel there, the big one. Do you have any questions so far?"

"Nope."

Men like Ali appreciate no-nonsense business and love their partners more if they speak less and think even less.

Bruno's party rocked all night. Few couples, villagers, and volunteers lurked around dead ash pits. They were in that sickly phase between last night's drunkenness and today's sobriety. The dungy piss mist that greeted me every morning dusted the whole scene until the plain-white of the sun, the big white bully in the sky, soaked it up and cooked me tired. I can't believe I was ever in love.

*****

In his topless jeep inside the smoldering parking of the hotel Gustave wished me well with Ali. A certain third world naiveté akin to desperation made Ali's goblin generosity seem like a wise and beneficial offer to bank on. But I knew I was taking my life's biggest risk for the sake of art and infamy. I saw all the deadly and deranged potential but I decided the payoff, this book, was worth the risk.

Being with Ali and the gang kept my imagination on the brim of a smoldering volcano because never did I feel too cozy. I had to connect an array of covert dots inside a world I only had assumptions about. Most of my formal education on organized crime was gleaned from entertainment.

I steadied my fluttering nerves when I approached Ali in the lobby. He quietly gestured for me to step back through the door while he followed. His Range Rover was parked in front of the golden hotel with his four men inside. I crammed myself into the cool leather interior and was greeted with silence.

At the wheel, Ali called back to me that the destination was outpost Village الحياة, populated with more Muslims than Christians and fostering a less French touch than an Arabic tinge. We drifted eastward and the ride reflected my back home experiences of going down I-696, but now I was in the company of humanoid sticks of dynamite crowding me. Ali drove while Arthur rode shotgun. I shared the back with Andre and Cox. The now unnerving hum of rubber on road gurgled the breakfast I skipped. Outer silence, inner turmoil was my anatomy.

Ali checked on me via the rear-view mirror – something I would do. The little tricks of soaking in the scene and assessing all the angles stealthily are my forte as an artist. He was obviously creative but not an artist. And the streaking glimmers of reflection I saw of him tickled and intrigue me. As we arrived around the low squared houses and blocky buildings the dumbbell pressure of too much weight and not enough strength seeped into my blood.

The anticipation of Ali's little test made fear paralyze me as if I was bitten by a snake that squirted adrenaline instead of poison, could I run away or bail out the back if I messed up? Would he hunt me down if I failed or fainted? Only a jerk like me would be in this situation. I felt the weight of silence like just before the first ever nuclear bomb test.

I knew how I arrived here but was this really me? My whole shitty life leads to a tightrope walk over Hell's lake? Yes, this is what assholes call Karma – the word needed when life finally tackles you and calls you out for all of your bullshit. My mind was so hectic playing with the possibility that I forgot the tangible was already here.

No warning – here's the hotel. Get out. Wait for Ali first. Be Calm. Look cool. The sun is your friend. No one knows anything anyway. Walk beside and behind Ali but not in the middle. Don't scratch your shoes. Look more casual. Walk faster. Glance around casually. Don't frown. Adjust those eyebrows. Sway more. Keep pace. Walk through the door like the rest, you belong here too. Stop – Ali stopped. Wait, now follow without question. Ignore the odor from the stalls, forget the irritating white lights.

"A white businessman with an imitation alligator briefcase sits in the lobby on a bench with his face in his phone. Get his wallet and bring it to me."

"Okay."

One of the men, Cox, inspected something on his dumb-phone at the sink behind Ali. I swooped out with the butterflies blending inside. The briefcase slept beside one calf on the floor.

The man sat glued to his phone. Approaching the desk I asked the woman for a pen and piece of paper. As I walked away I intently scanned the hotel sheet and tripped over myself, falling across the lap of the lonely tourist.

"I'm sorry, I'm so sorry..."

Grabbing his left shoulder to support myself back up and apologizing, I pointed to the floor, "I don't want to see anyone else get hurt, someone needs to clean that spot up. Again I'm sorry..."

Back in the bathroom, I handed Ali the tan leather wallet, "here you go."

After he counted the money and inspected its contents he handed it to the silent assistant at the sinks, Cox, who pocketed it inside his grey cargo jacket.

"Nine hundred Euros and some cards. You did a good job. Let's have drinks. Where do you like to go?"

"The World Away Bar."

"Let's go."

Cox left his jacket and wallet inside the rover when we got out to go in. I felt like a proud son knowing I earned Ali's trust and validated his assumptions of me. Obviously, the money was nothing to them.

I love making people feel like they know me. I love making people think they're smarter for having assumed, just by looking at me, that I'm smart. Arthur, Ali, and I drank face to face while the other two drank and blabbed behind us. We played the eye game very well. Our stares were synced perfectly. We looked at each other between looking away without catching each other. Arthur sucked on a non-filtered Lucky Strike – something I had not done in five years. I envied his reasons for smoking; my old ones haunted me now.

A swamp-black beer for me and three syrupy shots for Al. He took the conversational high ground after two, "What do you want to be remembered for? What are your ambitions now?"

I measured my false response with lipping the lather from my upper lip, "After my death, I want to be remembered for my writing, not that I worked hard to love someone."

Shot three, "Now that you work with me not many people will know you, trust me. You can't write about this. So what book do you want to be remembered for?"

Oh, the gurgling hubris in my artistic core. "I want to write a book about something big, something that covers a lot of important bases with me in the center. I'm not sure yet."

I would never betray you or anyone, Al. Come on; do you think I'm a sneak, a worm, a coward? Do you think I'm a real author? I'm just some throw-away with a swelled head from years of dreaming. And I just played dumb to get you off my back.

"How about you? What do you want to be remembered for?"

He flags the waiter down for three more, "A generous businessman and patriot. I ask because I'm a little weak with my vanity and I'm curious about how others deal with theirs."

"Me too. I love finding what people fear most, where they haven't tramped and all the blank spots in their thinking from neglect, and why they neglect it."

"That's very smart. The more you see, the more you map."

I spiced the exchange with adding a red-hot herb to the topics, "Have you killed anything besides animals?"

A groaning chuckle from his liquored throat then, "Anyone who knows themselves knows they're capable of murder."

I tipped my glass to him, then to my mouth.

"How about you? They said you were a big-time hunter in Bruno. They said you talked about it a lot, about back home and things."

"I've only killed animals. But I agree with you, anyone can become a murderer. I think life has made that choice for us regardless of how we feel about killing."

"I like that. I saw you knew what you were doing when I first noticed you. You're a good man."

"Thank you. You're a better one. Just know I respect you more than anyone else I've come across, because of your character and personal success."

He kicked the shot back and called to order. Most of life is a form of military and the better behaved you act the more the brass coddle you. He ordered three whiskeys for me and the dish he insisted was the best in town. As he babbled I was considering chucking the meat if it were part of the meal but I forced my insides to steer clear of the fear of any dumb speed bumps I might encounter. If I think too much it could all be bungled. He'll explain what he needs from me and I need to vomit little commentary, his kind like it that way.

In so many ways I was already seeing my dirty double in him. Of course, he didn't really see me and I liked it that way. We continued on about our respective homelands. His speech wasn't the rambling treadmill of thought that Mark's was. Ali spoke sparingly and devastatingly. And a mutual understanding showed through the motions of our interaction. We both saw that we knew the bad in the world.

"It doesn't surprise me that you got away with the Mickey Mouse stuff back home."

"I won't go on about it because I see you know the same things, but it was so much easier to live there if you broke the rules. You can get a lover, get money, and make friends if you just go for it your own way. Before I began I learned how to separate lies from truth and feeling from acting."

A slow nod of churning approval rolled to me, "I'm glad you understand the importance of making your own rules, refining rules of the world to fit your advantage. But only use that creativity when we have a job to do. Do not become disobedient to me and the others - I will only tell you one time."

He eyed the bottom of the tumbler for the ice that wasn't there, "how else did you survive back home?"

"I've forged documents since I was a kid, either to get through school, cheat the courts or get help from the government. I've sold drugs when they would come into my life, stuff like that - nothing big or impressive, just risky. But I think we're all more reckless when we're super young when rules are discovered only after going too far."

His wide mouth opened around the black beard and showcased that hallucinatory tooth beside the row of other stained headstones.

He kept grinning as he laid the bills down on the check. Back inside Rover Ali sat at the wheel and announced to me, "We're going to Mao. We're dropping off a shipment there then we will head out after we make another stop."

My ringing stomach, my necklace of sweat and a ton of self-doubt anchored me down. Rover roared down the road after Al peeled out and hit the open asphalt like a child in a bumper car high on hate.

The subtle, helpful distractions came from the purr of the rubber and the breeze of the air conditioning. The other white guy besides me was the inbred mongrel with too much edge and no filter: Cox. He twitched his giraffe neck at anything real or imaginary on the road. He must have been the English equivalent of the 'tourist decoy' Ali longed for. I was the American decoy, god bless me.

He belched a few words and half sentences like, "fucking desert." "This is it, the reward for being smart about shit." "Everyone, dirty cunts." Missing brain cells as well as coordination, he bumped my thigh with his knee the whole ride. Saying he was pub-trash was complimentary. Back home is the equivalent of a pick-up truck driving father of a bastard litter, wearing a beard on the face for manly assurance and a hat on the skull for the insecure baldness. Old clichés.

Rolling through the beginning of time I got the feeling that a nuclear apocalypse or a frosty mammoth meteor, even a dragon's ominous weather forecast would not affect this world. If I died here, I died at home. I assumed the others held a light version of my poetic insight of the locality. And I love knowing I'm always king of poetic insight no matter where I land.

For two hundred and fifty miles no Bruno's appeared. Ali conferred with his pale chemo buddy from the old island, "Cox, give me gum."

"Yeeh, here."

My English counterpart slithered around and nudged the gum on my hand to give.

"Can I have a piece?"

"Yeeh."

Minty latex squished in my mouth. "Thanks."

"Yeeh." His buzzed scalp scratched the glass as he settled to sleep.

Mr. Tan-man, riding shotgun, did busy work on a map while plugging coordinates into the GPS on the dash. And here I am, me myself and I all alone inside my space. Not once did Ali peer my way, but his sneakiness wasn't above my suspicion. I already knew the bearded serpent was constantly eyeing me. But what can I really tell from snake eyes?

Chapter 8

During the ride, Mao quickly morphed into a diminutive third world oasis. Cox coddled the tinted glass with his milky, sinewy face and moaned like a worried woman in a bad dream. The Tan-man (Arthur) burbled to Ali and Al nodded before making a sharp right onto a yellow sick road. Bump, jump, thump.

Like in N'Djamena, but on a smaller scale, the single path sprouted side streets; flat Pueblos, junk vendors, stray animals and spindly natives roving with stick appendages and colored garbs. Few basket-headed women weaved through the dusted streets.

The arctic winds of the air conditioning seemed surreal opposed to the conditions behind the centimeter of glass. Ali paused at each intersection to inspect the buildings. Tan-man pointed right, so we went right. We slowly stopped at a place labeled black paint 'تنظيف المنزل' or as it read below in English, 'Cleaning House'. I knew the front was a front. Back home so many cleaning businesses and rehabilitation clinics were decoys hiding crime within. A riveted black iron door waited.

Tan-man dialed on the phone outside, spoke low, and open sesame... Ali, of course, holding my left shoulder as we stepped in together. Decades-old vacuums and floor buffers with straw brooms sleeping around the abandoned shop was all I saw officer, I swear. The dated third world shined with the old heat of inefficient light bulbs. Behind the brown workbench of a counter rested an ancient cash register and the dealer; young and silent.

Ali slid a dirty white scrap across the counter, the dealer palming it after they greeted each other in Arabic. Inspecting the inspector inspect it looked to me, with the earthy gunk stuck to it, like ivory was a petrified plant you plucked from the dirt like a marble turnip. Two fingers wide and one finger long, the swarthy young man branded with gaudy fashion logos tumbled the old bone under his nose then probed the crevices with the edge of his liver-colored tongue. He and Ali shared more Arabic.

The owner nodded and huffed while handing the scrap back – scrap, what a term for something that cost $5,000. I questioned the tremors of his young fingers before stuffing them into his jean pockets. Ali rotated and pointed to the door while I stood on my mark: an invisible teeny white star under both shoes for my cameo.

The owner buzzed a silent alarm and the iron door resembling the side of an ancient submarine unlatched itself for the pushing. We three watched the other three play watchman and transporters. Two moved a wood crate from under the back seat. It was the size of a coffee table with cleaning supply brands stenciled on all sides. Cox pulled the door shut when they stepped back inside. The dealer locked the door from the desk then turned around and pushed back the wall that displayed an array of cleaning products.

He flicked a light on above our heads and the unspectacular sight of crates with stenciled warnings and false labels lay inert at our legs. Dust, shadows and the heavy silent stillness of dead time invaded my skull and spun my brain around. Andre and Arthur placed the box at Al's cloth military boots. The freshman stayed frozen while the men crowbarred the wood-knotted lid. Under excelsior and kindly wrapped in Chadian newsprint lay the stacked rows of three-foot tusks. It was the smallest cemetery I'd ever seen.

This low-rent rat began molesting and sniffing the gift-wrapped bones. He went to a blind corner and emerged pushing a solid wood box over resembling our ivory box but marked with bold French and Arabic. We all watched him extract a large satchel hiding beneath newsprint. Ali unzipped the black bag and fingered the bills inside. The quick business partners shook hands and were off after a fair exchange.

Ali exited with me around his shoulder. Outside he started his confident and confidential speech, "See that went well." He took me to the driver's seat as the boys piled in, "most men would have killed that kid and sacked the ivory for themselves. But he is the little face man for a big boss - a very big boss. He's not as big as me, but still a threat if violated. And since the business is so efficient now we mark the items so we know where the ivory came from and where to trace it, like bullets and currency. Little numbers or symbols tell us if it came from a trusted dealer like me or some clown scheming for himself. My name, the mark I use, is now impeccable."

He leaned in to hush, "it is tempting to take all that money from that poor kid, but the men backing him are too powerful. My reputation cannot be jeopardized."

His man-to-man transparency worked a sneaky charm on me. The electrifying feeling of being part of something alien quietly jolted my nerves. But it was a foreign feeling my scrutiny spotted immediately so the antibodies of my character reigned down and held it at bay until I felt comfortable manipulating it for my advantage. Nothing enters me without my invading it to my advantage.

"Come on, we'll have dinner here then find a hotel or drive to somewhere better."

We continued our tropical break around town. I'd plucked out the sad truth somewhere in Bruno that almost all people come to Chad to pass through an annexed obligation between Niger and Cameroon. Back on de Gaulle Avenue, in the capital, where the WAB sleeps every night in a hornet's hive, even the stray NGO workers I spotted had dreadful candor and good-will resolve.

Even they didn't find the wealth and warmth I did in Bruno, behind the white walls of culture's blister. Just the kids, those hopping black flowers popping around my legs all animated with life, made coming to this avoided country worth all the money and popularity in the world. The Tan-man sweated inside his mold, "Andre, where do we go?"

The black bull beside me rattled words like a brimstone throw rug unrolling from the crown of a volcano. Ali halted in front of a grove of businesses when his eyes matched the words Andre bellowed. A hollow heroin hooligan on my right and a silent space rock hurtling through society dressed as a military junkie on my left.

Mao's best-reviewed café housed us five and a dozen locals – mostly young family's swaying in from temple to table on this holy Friday. And would you believe it, silent reader, Ali let me choose the table! Me! The boys followed my lead. Power, my silent reader, pure power! We'd entered a hub of hospitality and the few who looked at me smiled, seriously smiled at me.

It's a lot different than where I come from. I was anticipating an old west cantina where Wild Bob meets Wild Bill and their pistols decide which dummy walks away the better dummy.

Only humming honey bees blurbed beautifully together inside this warm hive. I couldn't spot one of their stingers and didn't try. Like our foster father, Ali netted our orders then relayed them to a beaming black beauty with notepad.

Ali nudged Andre when she left and Andre was all gentleman, he only acknowledged his attraction with a nod. Somewhere in his deranged, rotting cranium, I saw his vision of a homespun African queen galvanized to his backside as he storms back home across the plains from a fruitful day of elephant play. Her garbs fluffing in the simmering dusk as he boldly gallops towards more manhood.

He by far had the cleanest fantasies and romantic ideals among us five. Cox caressed his cell phone, scrolling through his own pictures (and holy cow what blatantly retarded things those must be). Tan-man uprooted the edges of his nails with a toothpick and eyed the kitchen while Ali and I waited with hands folded. We shared smirks and I did a small impromptu drum roll with my fingers. His face was fixed on my face and I recognized it as the silly stare before a polite interrogation. "How is your writing coming?" My hairs stabbed me inwardly with his tone of, 'I already know, I went through your bag and already read it...oh, sorry.'

"It's good, it's always wrong to talk about a work in progress but when I'm done you'll read it." I made damn sure to omit, 'I'll let you' or 'you can' or 'maybe'. "I doubt if it'll get published, but it doesn't matter. In the end, I'm just doing it for my amusement."

"What amusement does it bring?"

"Knowing I did have it, that I was the best and that I didn't waste my youth doing nothing. I had it and I proved it to myself if no one else."

"Unfortunately I do not know anyone in the publishing industry so I don't believe I could help you get it out there. But maybe if you're fine seeing it printed in China or India you'll allow me to help?"

"Honestly, at this point, I'm not at all opposed it."

"I could do that."

"We'll see."

Here comes the waitress somehow holding seven different platters on either arm.

"After this, we can go for a swim."

His childish itinerary was so silly and contrasted it killed me. 'Oh, let's go roller skating and get cotton candy at the slaughterhouse!' He began by dismembering steaming sheets of flatbread while eyeing the colored gunk it went with on the sides.

"I want to go to Lake Chad after this. It'll take a while but it's worth it. I haven't swum in a long time. You?"

"Years now, I couldn't swim in concrete. Last time I swam was back home, up north." Chew, nod, chew. The other's arched solemnly over their meals and shoveled the melted crayons in with fingers and arid flakes of Chadian bread. I joined in now, subduing the sulfuric scene in my stomach. The mellow dough lifted the warm blobs of color to my wet mouth. Yum!

I saw a sudden typhoon of thought wind in him - his face turning the color of a shark's belly. I let him eat until he had it all cataloged and ready to fire. Pick that tooth, suck that gum and smack that tongue.

"Seleka is thick in the Central African Republic. They own it now and are starting to spread here."

"I hate to sound so ignorant, but what or who is Seleka?"

"No, do not worry. You must know this to look out for them. They're much more dangerous than the poacher hunters. I avoid the Central African Republic because of them now. No one doing what we do can go toe to toe with them now and it would cost too much to be in good with them. Chadian peacekeepers gave their armbands to Seleka rebels, and Chadian troops are ambiguous, to begin with, so Chadian troops play both sides and are usually with Seleka. They work together.

"The sixteen thousand French troops stationed here in Chad informed everyone of this: the peacekeepers lying down to Seleka and now Seleka is slowly spreading its position. Even ex-Seleka rebels have started to deal ivory from houses. The business is being brought to that low level because of them. French soldiers are still arresting them over it. They're all scoundrels and dogs."

"How can I tell who is with Seleka?"

"Outside of the Central African Republic, where they're in uniform, you can't. Gangs are the norm here and no one knows who belongs to whom because unlike in your country, here in Africa and elsewhere we don't advertise our allegiances. We like getting away with it."

Oh, Ali. I know exactly what you're saying. I've been a most desirable counterfeit bill ever since I was in circulation.

"That's the secret key to my secret operation. I recruit only men I can trust, never women. I recruit them for other things." Queue wink, "And if one person goes rogue or doesn't fit in with the team – goodbye." Queue finger-gun firing.

My eyebrows went 'Yikes!' But no one, trust me, silent reader, no one scares me. Back home, if I was prone to depthless fear my life would have been over quickly. Sometimes I miss my dad. He taught me how to dance around bullies like Ali and survive. He never knew he did that for me but he did and I erect an insulting statue of ironic appreciation in his honor.

The other three goons seemed to sulk in their own world. This is the aftermath of mob mentality, of team sports. Ali too, like all leaders, was miserable but he could afford to always look the other way, with hubris and control, at the stars he wished were calling his name. He did look away when he saw his men in their mid-season slump. He busted up the dead silence with one hand to flag the waitress.

Lugging ourselves up and out we palmed our eyes at the offensive sun. Rover purred with the air conditioning blowing on us before we abandoned Mao, "Hey! Look."

Ali's glare waited for me in the rear-view and I shot my head around to look, "Oh, yeah…"

"See, Seleka is everywhere. Since they overthrew the Central African Republic they've rooted their small-time hoods in Chad and a few other countries."

Two French officers were courting a shamed native in cuffs. The officers read him his rights while he sat on the curb hanging his head. Two more officers carted a nightstand-size crate from the unmarked building.

"Don't worry, our friend has no chance of getting caught. That couldn't happen with us."

"What if they walked in on us dealing ivory?"

He reflected his possible reactions against the hypothetical scene, "if they didn't take our offer we'd just be finishing discarding them."

His hard pirate profile leered at the officers. He didn't plow away like I thought he might. When Rover rolled away Ali retracted into his brooding. The ride smoothed out our kinks, small as they were. The world was locked out and behind cool panes. Moving along all that earth welled up those pesky flashes of my past and made way for the eloping of time and discovery – the future. I love being a writer. I love knowing I'm the only one I know who's doing this with their life.

But I'm letting Africa's magic work wasted wonders on me. I'm just a man with too many hobbies. Africa sped on, so did we.

After four hours in, and clocking one hundred and twenty-five miles per hour since Mao, Al told me our itinerary, "hey, we're heading to Cameroon. We'll be out of Chad in a couple of hours. We're staying in Douala in the

New Bell district. We'll check into the Hotel Akwa Palace tomorrow."

"Good."

"You'll be disappointed by Lake Chad because it's getting soaked up by the changing heat. But it's fine, it's called Africa in miniature for a reason and there are plenty of coasts and lakes. I do believe you'll be shocked when you see Douala." And away his voice went. I finally felt ingratiated enough to succeed in sleeping away the remaining hours between the two dumb statues.

*****

Honk! The preternatural signals of Ali combatting buzzing traffic were tipped to me through half-light and half-consciousness.

Ali hushed to his side, "They act like all of Boko Haram was waiting in the middle of the street to be arrested. What is this?"

Honk number two! Honk number three, four, five, six, seven etc. We clotted on a misted freeway, all dusky gloom and tarnished lights breathing around us inside dense fog. The blemished beacons from skyscrapers and buildings showed a cliché sci-fi film of post-apocalyptic scenes. But of course, all sci-fi is cliché at this point.

The quick aggregate effect of not seeing the city whole, by being camouflaged by nasty elements, pissed me off. I hate bad inductions to new areas. I sat locked in a dark back seat with hundreds of crimson discs shrugging in my sore face. Long traffic on a shitty night.

Tan-man scribbled his forefinger on his phone and readjusted the GPS on the dash. Ali mumbled something intense but frivolous. My statues slept with their ears open and so did I. I'm one of the gang now.

*****

I kicked my manuscript when I was startled awake, scrapping the pages apart through my checkered duffle bag with one heel. The Hotel Akwa Palace, as I assessed my current position and seeable future, was going to be my interlude to regain my course as a writer with this story. I tried not letting my imagination fire visions and hopes about the what-ifs because anticipation is the root of disappointment.

Ali's gas/break action nudged me awake. My statues were upright and awaiting arrival. "You can stuff three America's in one Africa. I'm thinking of getting a jet for us all, but I need a trusted pilot."

My tonal 'yeah' died en route to Ali. The mist was the byproduct of the fleeting rain. Cameroon hopped like all modern cities hop in the dark – electric, mechanical and condensed.

Think of a ground level metropolitan city marked with luminous lights and iridescent shop fronts. The shaded outlines of the few high-rises stood before the background of a dirty copper sky. Somewhere between pollution, torrential weather and too much illumination (the humanized trifecta of any titanic city) was us. My attraction belonged to the blinking bloody bulbs dotting the high-rises of Africa's heroic metropolis.

Yes, Cameroon is the pride of a continent but I didn't want to indulge in culture. I wanted to awake over my papers, letting my mind splutter ink from my pinched fingers. And here I am, finally here letting the baggage of my mind unload properly. The Palace is grand enough for humble foreigners like me. The Wouri River sleeps like a black sea serpent tucked away for a night's rest before some bearded captain and his crazy crew conspires to kill it for the gold in its belly. Oh wait, that's us.

Gold is the past, ivory is the future. In the gilded lobby boasting giant crystalline chandeliers of lighted rectangles, Ali carefully selected who goes to which room. Now armed with an unmarked phone Ali allowed me to stay put in our shared bedroom. So here I am scrawling my gibberish with an Akwa fountain pen – really nice piece of homemade work.

I'll fill the red-rimmed tub after this chapter. Everything is red here; the black bellhop tucked in a fitting red suit, the black desk clerk wrapped in red synthetics, the red drapes skirting the oblong white façade, the red velvet pillows singing for my head, the red silk blankets burning for my body and the little red smear on the title page of this manuscript from a runny red paperclip. They all laugh at me. And I laugh right back.

Chapter 9

Douala woke with me as I watched the sun warm the red curtains. The solid windows kept the growing city acoustics outside. I felt pressured to fish my bleated thoughts for shape and structure when Ali rolled under his sheets - I had to be ready. And was my manuscript as naked as me?! Do I ask if Ali leafed its pristine pages? Will he give me the 'you better explain yourself' confrontation?

The red-rimmed shower shouted for my grit and it got a drain-full. Before I scrubbed with the soap and squeezed the shampoo in the steamy shower Ali was shifting and snoring through sensitive sinuses. 'Sss' goes the shower-head and 'Mmm' goes my throat. The tiled ceramic cooled my soaked feet from tub to sink and I made out Ali calling for breakfast – raspberry jam on rye with red pomegranate juice and a side of red meat. All this red made me feel caught and incriminated.

"We have a much busy day today." Al slammed his toast along the gnawed ridge of shitty steak and chewed away.

Almost losing whatever juices my stomach held I went to the divided window and spread one pane ajar. The Wouri River was alive now and slinked along, white crests breaking here and there on its dark lumbering surface.

"Come eat, we need to leave in fifteen minutes." I groped beneath my scattered sheets for my bag to get 'clothes'.

"I will, I just need to change first."

I locked myself in the bathroom and scrambled through this manuscript on the red trim of the closed toilet bowl. No traces of interference showed the bloody outline of the runny red clip wasn't smudged. This new scenario I'd landed in consumed my imagination and emotions entirely. It doused the thirst to consume new literature. So after whatever happened to me happened, I reasoned I would read again when all this is said and done.

"We need to leave now." Al's stern words grumbled through the timber. After zipping the bag shut I relieved my bladder and was off behind my new headmaster. The other three were lounging on two puffy red sofas in the lobby under one of the many chandeliers that hung like icebergs from a reachable heaven. I stood by them, alone, and didn't receive any warm signals from my comrades. Al checked us out with the clerk wrapped in cherry soaked stitching.

Facing the clean glass I timed my steps on sync with the others' as we marched out. We were a bizarre amalgam of intrigue. But groups and gangs are all so common in these parts. The gorgeous thing about running with criminals, thieves, and murderers around here is everyone only sees another group. Thankfully no one sees the person here.

Ali ignited Rover and ran us down to casino Kheops. We were meeting a faceless bigwig waiting in a spacious casino office. I only had to wait less than ten minutes to see him.

Ali called for me as we exited the vehicle and I took precise, measured steps of casualness to his side, "I have to tell you how to act in here. You and I will go in to meet my most impressive new business partner. He owns this casino and other buildings here. Just keep acting like yourself and you'll be fine. He'll like you. We have the same, uh...the same,"

"Sensibilities."

"I'm glad your English is better than mine."

"I'm a writer, remember?"

"Yes. And I'll read your book when it's done."

"That means a lot." He felt my upper spine in a gross sporting way.

Tacky and typical: the casino boasted one meek sign - an African shield with fat yellow block letters reading 'El Dorado'. Two fruit vendors chatted with night-walkers beside the neon mauve entrance. Being the most luxurious of African cities I did expect more than this pale edifice. But I'm a fool with building things up.

It seemed two stories tall and didn't have any big flashing lights snaking the surface like back home with their Americanized Greek theme. Inside, blue-topped tables marked in white lines, letters and numbers crowded the crowds leaking around in droves. Giant wooden pillars split at the top like broken bananas or axed lumber stood as obnoxious obstacles around everyone's shuffling. Polite croupier's formally dressed black women handled the money and fates of all the suckers.

Al stepped a few paces ahead and we entered a gold-plated elevator with three buttons for three floors. Al pressed the small lighted 3 when everyone was in. Ding! Swoosh goes the double doors. We walk off down a red-carpeted hall with one double black door at the end. Al hit the buzzer and open sesame again! All these magic doors got me panicked.

We strode halfway into the room and halted before a fifteen-foot wide desk. Behind the glossed black wood sat, then rose, a puffy Asian gnome fitted with a butler's suit wearing a faded crooner's haircut. He reminded me of a freaky little dictator. He and Al shared paws and greetings. The men beside me unhinged their stances and started fiddling with their phones. I moved my feet from here to there and fidgeted with my hands. Death's breath tickled my senses and I cranked my neck to see another little Eastern dictator sucking on a cigar. He crossed his calves in a bulbous black leather chair in the far right corner opposite his own delightful double.

The head goon, offering Ali a cigar, urged us all to sit in the swamp of brother chairs at our sides. Ali asked if the men could go downstairs and play some games. Shorty buzzed in a hostess that ushered them back downstairs. But Al waved me forward as the men followed lady luckless.

"Tiger, this is my new apprentice. I picked him up in a village in Chad. He's American."

My lean vice gripped the manicured paw of pillowed digits. "Hello." He only gave a nod and a wink.

The cigar sucker swooped down beside Al and me and the unofficial meeting began. There's no pep talk or college advice that primes one for a meeting with two criminal penguins and one solid elephant poacher.

Al twisted the Monte Cristo between thumb and forefinger as Tiger spit his game, "Ali, you know my business and my people - we are always looking for hunters and businessmen such as you. Nothing would make me and my partners happier than you doing business with us. We know you've fortified your operation into most of central Africa now. We have interests here, as well as India and back home in China. After this year's hunting season I would love to have you as a guest at my new home in India, and if everything goes well my permanent residence in China."

A drop of all noise occurred, landing into a sweeping silence as Ali considered. "I'm very open to doing business with you. We'll need to talk fine details tough."

"Of course."

Tiger beamed two chins my way and Al deflected, "He is my partner. He can listen."

Blob-zilla nodded slow and drank syrup colored whiskey from glasses with tinkling cubes.

"I trust you, Ali. That's the foundation for everything." Al agreed without speaking. Money makes the world spin, and it circulates better because of thieves. Without thieves, money wouldn't move as efficiently.

His sales pitch stomped on, "The hunting season, this hunting season, we would like to be your sole purchaser. We have prepared an outstanding offer that no one else can match."

"What's the offer?" The number split my brain. Ali played it supremely cool with a molasses nod and swift stroke of the beard. "Helping you and your people after making me such a generous offer would be beneficial for everyone involved. How will payment be made?"

Chubby crushed his cigar before it blacked out, "any way you feel most comfortable."

Ali scribbled a scribe on three-inch notepad paper and handed it off. Chunky chucked it in the polished baby bin after seeing the request. Al broke in to clarify, "a shipment that big will need protection at all times until it's gathered for sale. Could you lend me some of your men so I can to stow it all away somewhere discreet?"

"Oh, yes. You can store it here if you need."

"Ha, no. We'll work out a more discreet location before the hunt begins." Nasty nodded.

"My men are at your disposal."

"With your help, you can trust me when I say I will have it all in three months. I just may need a little more assistance with ensuring it."

"No problem."

Head shakes and smiles were shared. For me, that was the moment. Prior to Ali even, that was when I considered myself a poacher on paper and I wondered how I'd blundered so badly. Cops and robbers are one thing, but this really was life and death. I may never live to see middle age now that I signed up for this, with these people.

I felt if someone struck a match near me we would all blow. More than any other time in my life I reached a new brink of mania – either slip away or carry out this messy ordeal to sinister completion. I clung to the ladder, hoping I hadn't already eaten the first rung. Accompanied by the eager emperor penguins we landed back in the game room where Ali and I magically won ten thousand dollars in Cameroonian currency. See, all criminality is financed legally.

*****

Ali let the men play in the game room all night provided they didn't stray and make trouble across town. I followed the leader. The little, stolen instrument in my checkered duffle slept untouched and I sighed the relief of the grateful criminal – grateful not to god or circumstance but to that validation of your intuition. I knew Ali wanted to trust me and didn't want to read my work and certainly not skim through my belongings. He wanted to like me and I couldn't help but like him despite who and what he was.

I sometimes love murderers. I love their awful world and how they live inside it. I love how I love everybody, especially myself. I could never turn my back on myself.

I zipped it back inside the side compartment, under this swelling manuscript. Ali was on the horn with a bank somewhere and I decided to shoe-gaze out the windows. Douala was all clockwork from above and the sight made me want to go straight; get a job, pay taxes and slit art's throat. But who am I to act like everyone else?

Al clicked off and ordered more room service. After fifteen minutes of me dazing and him examining the screen of his laptop, dishes of red bean chili were placed on the big low table by a bellhop who bowed at the giant tip. Al started digging in, waiting for me to sit two feet away and chomp in his face. The chili only had sauce, red beans, and herbs - thankfully no meat.

I ate and tried savoring it despite my nerves. A teeny heart-colored mess kept smudging on his moon-tooth like acid rain hitting a windshield on Venus. There it is; there it goes between his chattering and chewing. His candor said either of us could start talking so I got brave and began fishing, "when will we begin the hunting season?"

His runny acid tooth got wiped clean by his lips, "tomorrow. We've been preparing for three weeks so I want one day here to relax and have a short holiday. It's very tough out there and I want to have a day to remind me of what I work for." I tried adding legitimacy to my next phony statement, "this isn't the capital of the world but it's still very nice."

He paused and gave me a 'let-me-let-you-in-on-a-little-worldly-secret' look, "fuck culture. There is no capital of the world and I'm never going to claim one by being a cynic. The capital of the world is wherever you are." Almost half apologetic for his slight outburst he asked if I got lonely in Africa away from home.

"The author is the only person who gets stronger with loneliness."

After a nod and a shrug, he was back to his beans. Something in my mind is very adept at manipulating imagery, constructing and obliterating the boundaries and having breakfast with an elephant poacher the caliber of Ali felt like a dirty job interview you had to ace. In total, I only relaxed around him three or four times and this wasn't one of them. I guess his sensitivities were slithering on broken glass today with loads of pressure; new hunting season approaching in less than twenty-four hours, new business deal (the biggest), my future as newest member etc. He handled it impeccably.

I was so intrigued and impressed that I honestly wanted to know more about him, "do you have any family?"

"I have one sister. She married a merchant in Turkey. He's from a little town called Kars. I believe he exports vegetables. We seldom see each other. Do you?"

"I only have a mother now. My father died of a heart attack, that's why I came here. I couldn't stand home anymore and needed to do something constructive with my life." He hung his face low into his dish. "How did you get into the ivory business?" I felt such a fraud calling it a business and not a holocaust.

"My old friend. We were soldiers in the Egyptian army. He got involved with white gold and I followed. After we made our first fortune he was murdered." Face to dish again. "That's tough. I lost my best friend a few years ago. I found in order to stop thinking of the big things you have to think of the little things and vice versa."

He nodded an approving frown at his beans. Damn, how can I get my new boss to get on an open track with me? "Do you have a girlfriend or wife?"

"Relationships always show me what I try to hide best: that I'm the worst person I know." His brows sprung with faux surprise. He followed up after a few minutes, "no one will ever give you the truth about yourself, though. You have to find it yourself. And remember this – sex is the beginning of the end of all relationships."

"Yeah, but only if you're bad at it."

"..."

No! Fuck! I hit rock bottom like a dead bottle rocket! He hunched over his beans again. After the platter was cleared he asked if I had read anything good in the news. I noted the three papers strewn beside plates.

"Something, some new scientific theory about the universe, our reality, being a hologram. They say maybe this is all a hologram or a reflection of an alternate universe – a simpler one. That's why we're so damn limited. I'm sure somewhere we can do all the things we really dream about. Somewhere, I'm sure, there is a more complete and dynamic version of ourselves and it's not heaven – it's somewhere else, and if we ever see it, it will laugh in our face. Heaven will come be to known as an insidious one-way mirror, just watch."

He only stared at me. Fuck! It felt like I was back home inside a stuffy righteous house. The dad was disappointed that I didn't bring something new to the home.

Then he shocked me with a line that upstaged my whole theatrical effort, "just remember this: sex is like violence - it doesn't matter. It only matters what happens before and after. Trust me and forget about holograms and limitations. You need to be practical in life."

I gave up. Moving the plates aside he arranged his laptop and phone in their places to have a crack at the day's work. Despite his original intentions with the day, good criminals are never lazy.

I eased back and plopped on the angry red sofa – my back towards Ali. I spied a few frozen vultures atop the antennas of the high-rise across the way. They were waiting like a family of feathery vampires in the city sun, getting toasty and recharged before more scrounging.

"They're getting ready for their hunt, too." Al dropped his words like a bulldozer dumping stones.

"Where do they come from? How do they get into the city from the desert?"

"There's a zoo a few miles away from here. They live there and have hunting spots around the city. I despise zoos." "I do too, but how come you do?"

"I loathe animal sadists. Torture and confinement are much more cruel, primitive and barbarous than killing the thing. To get a desired reaction over an animal is pathetic – just kill it if it's your frightened slave. Don't be a pervert, be a man. All animal sadists are perverts. They long for the master, slave relationship. They all long to be respected and followed, and not mildly or all at once, but like god because everyone shuns them. We're not leaving the hotel today so make yourself comfortable. I don't mind if you go to the pool or bar but stay in the hotel. And answer your phone if one of us contacts you."

"Of course. I'll have a drink in the pool after I take a dip at the bar."

"Good."

Pocketing a little black notebook I'd brought from home to jot my fragmented ideas on, Al called me back before I let the door click shut, "We will come back after the hunting season is over. I'll show you how great Cameroon is in its entirety when you have nothing but money and time."

"Good."

His head was back at his work before I walked out. With impending horror at my iterating future, I walked to the bar three floors below – taking the acrid elevator all by my lonesome. Who should I see slumped on the bar but Cox? His anemic shape contorted beneath the leather jacket with who knows how many drinks shooting through his veins. I somehow decided to chat him up, to experience his true self with the liquor working its charm.

"Hey Cox, buy you a drink?"

His scruffy dome turned halfway to utter, "Yeeh, if you want."

I spotted the bartender, "Hey Buster, get me the blue Johnny Walker. Nothing's too good for my rich cousin. Just add it to his bill." He sat slumped before the raised television, engaged in emotional battle as the soccer game crawled along. I noticed the abbreviated teams, Man. Un. and Wes. Hmp.

"Who are you pulling for?"

His voice wandered back, "Manchester."

"Here."

"Thanks."

After forty-five minutes of play and no score he slinked round in the high metal stool, "so what're you doing with your paycheck when we're done?"

"I'd like to travel more and explore the world, maybe get a job somewhere else."

When he sucked the drink down his neck's tendons and arteries welled with strain and relief.

"Ali's upstairs. I left him to his work."

"Yeeh…"

"Yeah, how long have you been doing this?"

Sip, stare, think, speak, "two years. I was in the army, then prison, then here."

"What were you in prison for?"

Sip, stare, think, speak, "rape. You been to prison?"

"I'm trying to break out now." I colorfully equated my hellish life back home to prison.

"Yeh…whatever."

"…I can tell Yannick is good with technology."

"Yeh, he's our head geek. I wish Manchester could win this game."

"Yeh."

"Where are you from?"

When I said it he tipped his glass, "nice area. How's the blight holding up?"

"Better than ever. What are you doing with your money?"

"Eh, dun know. Think I'll go back to Holland."

Holland has lots of edible stars and I could imagine a bumbling black hole like Cox sucking up the hard work of all those favored sluts.

"Do you have any family?"

"Nope."

This interrogation couldn't be any worse if it was done by the police. Cox had nothing to give drunk or stone sober. The game scrolled on and he drank and drank and there he goes!

He buckled two feet from the bathroom and the bartender and I hooked his arms to the sink inside. I pretended to know what to do by just propping the dope up and slapping water across his ratty face.

"Eh! Eh!"

I slowly released my grip while he wobbled on his numb legs. He began rinsing his face at the sink while we exited. The black bartender in red silk vest and black silk dress shirt poured me a complimentary shot for the gross job of handling a swine like Cox. We had decency and heart so in such rare company it demanded a warm-hearted gesture like a complimentary shot.

He smiled his pearly whites behind the honey-colored liquid, "Cheers."

"Cheers." Down goes the gas, up comes the fumes. "Another?"

"Yes, thanks." I never ask for another, I never shove my luck down anyone's throat. "Does that happen often here?"

"Yes, all the time here."

"Sorry." He pushed my sympathy away and poured me half a shot. "Thanks. How's Lake Chad looking now?"

He contemplated the lake, "very good. Are you going?"

"No, my friends don't want to."

"Why?"

"I'm not sure. They said something about it shrinking and drying up now."

"No, it's still very big. You should go see it if you're here. Only if your friends are terrorists would they have any reasons not to go."

"What do you mean?" I theatrically engaged him with the slow inhalation of my drink.

"The C.A.R., Chad, Cameroon, Libya, Niger, and Nigeria all agreed to fund a joint military program to stop gun sellers and terrorists around Lake Chad. A lot of criminal things happen there so they have to protect it."

"Yeah … my friends are just here with me on vacation. They're not criminals."

"That's good to hear, I hope you're all enjoying your stay. Our elite special forces are hunting Boko Haram at the northern border with Nigeria. You should tell them to avoid those areas; it's a lot of police." I casually pointed and he tilted old dependable for me again.

"What is the special forces team called?"

"BIR or Rapid Intervention Battalion. The president declared war on Boko Haram in Paris at a summit. Radical Islam is trying to progress here in Cameroon."

"Back home, where I'm from, we have more Muslims in my state than all of Cameroon but none of them are radicals or extremists, and they live peacefully with Jews and Christians. There's never been one act of terror or threat. Why do you think that is?"

He studied my question like a hard-pressed mathematician, "that's interesting. I guess it's all about how people live, not where they live. You know?"

"Oh, I know."

By the end of his charming chatter, I thought I had met the only decent acquaintance in the continent besides Mark Hubble. And speaking of that jolly gentle giant, I needed to use my new untraceable phone to contact him. I still had his back home address in my little black notebook scrunched beside this manuscript. I knew what I wanted by now, I had formulated the first sneak peeks in my mind in Bruno.

And even a bit before that I had the desire to go off and make the world a better place using my unique sensibilities and devilish logic. My father, rest his life, passed on a legacy he would have wanted aborted if he could see me now, but part of this effort is my sick way of making myself proud to be his son. "Where's the pool?"

"It's near the roof. Take the elevator up to floor three."

"Thank you."

He waved goodbye with my bill rolled under his thumb. Ding! Out comes me like a snake from a cage and I slink my body towards the nearest body of water. Sunshine and top-shelf liquor is all-weather beatitude for what ails me. When I saw the rumbling blue aqua I imagined I was a well-dressed English consul slipping away in a remote village in rural Mexico with a strychnine bottle gripped in one hand.

I love myself. No one was around the pool on this day but an old maid of indeterminate ethnicity hunched here and there to sweep the few mildew clothes into a clear garbage bag for the lost and found.

The phone rattled in my right pocket. A text came through from Ali, "where are you?"

"At the pool, will you go swimming?"

"Yes. Give me a minute."

The maid left while high atmospheric winds swept down on me from the sky. I just lay helpless and hopeless under the pressures of life and surrendered to it all in the cradle of my chair while waiting for my friend. There goes some more time. Here comes an animal terrorist. There I go inside the minted blue body. Here comes the terrorist to join me, wetting his beard. And here comes another dreaded exchange because here I am.

Chapter 10

Our sleek white plane swam over the rolling horizon. I watched a world of sand reel out into eternity below. It seemed like we would never reach the end of the earth. I relished the feeling of being a tiny bubble frozen inside a pressurized can while flying in the plane. From the window, nature showed steamy patches of clouds floating above a hash-colored world with its little animals stationed here or sprinting there. Ali sipped mineral water in a grey fabric chair beside me.

He studied maps on his laptop and occasionally scrutinized the scene outside the window, though I thought he was just getting a sneaky view of me out of the corner of his peepers. Cox and I started drinking the champagne because we were the real cowards on board. The champagne gave my nervous system a light alcohol steam bath. Al said we wouldn't shoot today; we scout, track and plot the hunt. I promised myself, to stop my sanity from slipping, that not one of my shots was going to hit an elephant no matter what the price.

I jabbed my left calve with my new right boot – newly purchased for me in a military surplus store in Cameroon the day before the flight, and I wanted to bruise myself for not slipping away before this. I hoped Ali and the men wouldn't be too fed up with my lack of abilities in the field. If all we're eating is hunted meat and no vegetation because we're in the goddamn desert than I'm fucked. I can't choke that shit down. 'I'm not hungry guys, I got full on fear back there.' 'I'm not hungry guys, all of this elephant gutting has made me sleepy.' More champagne anyone?

I went from washing my horror to wanting to black out and not deal with these paranoid projections in the African sky. Through drunkenness, I imagined that after we landed I would find relief inside a bleary hangover under the bone-crushing compressor of the African sun.

*****

Here is Garamba National Park. All I remember seeing from the window were thousands and thousands of acres of eclectic landscapes. I'm sure you've seen plenty of photos and footage so fill the gaps in for yourself. We had flown into the Democratic Republic of Congo unauthorized while I was sleeping. Apparently, Tan-man and Ali had set up a Ugandan Military helicopter to be waiting via earth-patch helipad somewhere in the open where no rangers, scientists or tourists go.

The transfer went fast and efficiently as the warm wet pressure of the African summer coagulated me further into a vacationer's hell. In the helicopter, Ali explained via headset that the ivory business was becoming more militarized and not to jump at the sight of armed militants or soldiers or people who appear to be soldiers and anyone who might deal ivory which could be anyone now. The previous two decades was kids' stuff compared to the new epic elephant slaughter happening today.

This was my first hop in a helicopter and the pumping blades beating over my brain through a helmet of composite all seemed like experiencing a new amusement park trap. I thought of the old Vietnam stories my father repeated my entire life back home. I daydreamed of the films I was now sharing a scene with in real life. The feeling of finally being human and just having a new experience all kept jumping back to me. I did feel special that it was me in this spot, and not some other nobody. After all, I have ambition with this book and maybe if my most triumphant dream comes true you'll know why I was glad it was me, too.

The whoosh of the chopper spun so fast that it streamlined into a dull monotony of hollow baseball bats swinging by my head. After getting settled, I had looked at our crew all buckled and helmeted in like a kid's toy filled with GI Joe's. I felt for the cycloptic visor on my helmet and threw it down when we entered over a grassy plain with the sun screaming in our faces. Ali's words of garbled electricity shocked my ears as he collaborated with Yannick.

We were swooping into a section sheltered by diamond thick foliage with all the comforts of a free range before us. When the two-tone destination came into sight Ali yelled through our helmets, "People who say getting there is half the fun haven't gone anywhere!"

I saluted with one thumb when he smiled to me at his cramped side. Down we go. That nervous plunge your heart takes when it spits up your throat got me and I wondered if it got anyone else. After enduring the few seconds of weightlessness as we dropped we were down and out. Ali began his scoutmaster's role by pointing and telling the others to do this or that here and there.

He looked very proficient and professional ordering the men around, all against the chest-high elephant grass rippling behind. "Will it be fine in this wind?" Al quipped over one shoulder as Yannick tinkered with a plastic toy extracted from a black duffle.

Tan-man sized the sky and scrutinized the winds from his stylish crouch, "Yes, this model is better than the last. I have these too, so no more monitor."

Cox and Andre stepped long and soft into the green blades towards the brown forest. Their heads and shoulders were swallowed by the grass the deeper they got. Al unpacked a pair of military binoculars from one silver and black case and studied the whole horizon. No signs; smoke, gunfire, people, animals or vehicles were spotted. He slung the piece around his neck.

Tan-man snapped the toy together and uncoiled a skinny black wire adjoined to a visor and headset.

"Can I do anything?"

Al rested his forearm on my shoulder and contemplated the green and blue meridian before us. Like a father setting his child up on his birthday with one last secret gift he grinned and pointed to it. Animated Ali – you're so good to me. I hunched down to placate my boss. I knew nothing of these military toys used to annihilate humans. I only glanced at Santa's little killer while Tan-man snapped the final pieces together – batteries included.

Overhead Al gave me the backstory to it, "a Canadian company just started making these this year and I got my hands on the first batch. Israel is in line to purchase most of the lot. But these will be available to civilians now. I'm the only one who uses them for this."

"It's genius."

"We send it out for miles and see what's out there so we can track and map everything. It's the most useful thing we've done so far."

"It's very genius."

"I think the intense genius I have for this will be mimicked by other poachers but always remember I was the first."

And he dotted his declaration with a rise in his voice, showing how silly and sincere he was. And being under this ghoul showed me an angle of my character I could finally understand; I was really doing all of this death-stepping for knowledge and my own interpretation of our world. I desire more than anything a complete portrait of this thing called life before it's over. And I want it told my way.

Stupid as the ambition is, I want to try my best and at least mold my experience into salable dreams. So Tan-man raised the drone fifty feet above. The thing had four little black plastic blades like the mini-fans you used to cool yourself off with in the summer, assuming you were a child who got his toys from the dollar store too. Al agrees with nobody that it's perfect.

"Here," he swiped the visor and headset from beneath Tan-man's planted feet and let me cover my eyes with it. An HD sweep of the raised sight made me feel like I was stunned at the theaters with a grandiose movie engaging me in the dark. My head moved with the camera when Yannick shifted the drone right and left.

Tan-man noted somewhere outside my new world, "Don't move your head, it doesn't help. Stay still." My mind was tricked and I forgot I didn't need to move anything; the drone is your new eyes. I heard myself say to the floating vantage, "it looks incredible. I've never seen the world like this."

Ali was all smiles when I removed the headset. He took it and tried it on.

"Go a mile north."

I copied Tan-Man's silence in waiting for Ali's dictation.

"Go east now."

After being on guard for fifteen long minutes, "Okay, let's move it three miles south."

That stupid urge all men get when we're inside nature too long began creeping up in me. I was now a cat ready to fetch a bird in my teeth at the first sign of anything. I just wanted to run, explode and scream all around this place. Mother Nature is still the best amusement park.

Andre and Cox waded back to us through the grass. By their candor, I saw an altercation had taken place somewhere. Andre shook his stone head while Cox stood astray from the team. The sleeping helicopter began whistling and whizzing behind us. A Chinese pilot saluted us while the grass flattened and we lost our hairdos and hearing. My heart nearly fell through my rectum.

We're really alone now. A sinister silence strode into my marrow and stayed a while. After the fear said, 'I'm staying. Do what you want.' I thought maybe I'll finally understand the importance of teamwork. Cox zipped his camouflaged windbreaker, assuming a lanky mask of starving angst on his bony face. Andre loaded the rifles, bullet by bullet, clip by clip. Snap, click, cock.

A .458 Winchester magnum fixed with shock absorbing butt, a 400-yard scope and vented compensator sleeping at the mouth of the barrel was handed my way. I unlocked the bolt to check the pen-size cartridge as to show them I was competent with weapons. I peered through, stupidly, only to see a haze of lima bean grass two feet away but magnified at 400 hundred yards. Ali's silent guiding hand raised the barrel for me to focus the scope at the trees.

What spooked me most, as what always does, is what wasn't said as opposed to what was. I assumed we would use our phones to quietly communicate when hunting. Ali took a PKM and one FN Herstal automatic pistol for a sidearm. The rest got AK's and G-3's. I'm also assuming I got the only big game rifle because of my experience back home in rich forests with a 30.06.

But how I loathe guns now. Cradling this fifteen-pound piece of stupidity on my back wouldn't be warm cake. I wanted to test Al's knowledge, real knowledge, of this place's history.

I prodded, he gave way, "foreigners have been decimating elephants for decades, more than a century now. White gold was one of the primary reasons King Leopold turned Congo into his personal fief in the late nineteenth century. He helped pave the way for Congo going to crap and letting us get away with this now."

Oh, I had to tickle myself, "Yes, a timeless novel was written about it. I think it proved the worst side of ourselves is timeless." And hopefully, this stinking manuscript will prove that old heavyweight correct.

"I'm sure it's good. Let's move now then we'll set up camp five miles in." Arthur unclipped the drone and neatly packed it back into its bag. Slinging the maple wood stock of the .458 round my upper spine I began politely marching in the middle of our human chain through streamers of snapping grass.

The isolation of being trapped in a wispy maze didn't get manic or phobic. When my mind envisioned a tiger or leopard pouncing in from the sides I just remembered we're all armed. With only nature's breath talking overhead, I realized this was a job like anything else. They took it as seriously and as responsibly as a union member back home working an assembly line at an auto factory.

But of course, we would have to take it seriously now: to keep from losing the elephants, the money, the weapons, our health and our lives. I hadn't shaved since Cameroon and now I seamlessly slipped into the man's man role of big game adventurer, hunter extraordinaire and any other bullshit title dick-less cowards' use that lust after blood.

Conceding that writing this chapter of the experience was the easiest, and daresay most fun, makes me more of a criminal in my blackest depths than what we eventually did. You'll see my whole value system on full display soon enough, silent reader.

Mile two, mile three, four, five, six! 'We're going a full ten miles in. Drink and eat as needed. No trash!' Al's words buzzed in on our phones at once causing us to check as one. This endless grass maze had no exit and even a reverse trek towards the entrance felt pointless like we'd lost the key to our infinite prison. My whole futile life, naked like a balloon let loose from nature's invisible, cruel hand.

After the six-mile mark, the meat of my feet felt like wet socks. We didn't wear real leather because of its sinister attraction. Motivation replaced time here. For an entire mile, I let the green streamers slap my face as we brushed through. Mile seven, eight, nine, ten came and went without any sense of time, only motivation.

Only when Al's words rumbled in our pockets did we stop at a clearing in the grass about fifty yards round. Arthur began snapping the drone together again to scan the area in a five-mile radius. "We'll set up camp tonight, and tomorrow we'll go another ten miles west of here. We'll stay clear of the ivory coast because there's no more ivory there."

"The irony coast..." All eyes panned me with no interest.

Al continued, "...I'll have a jeep waiting for us that Tiger's men will send. Once we get to the plains the game is on. But if life smiles on us today or tomorrow we'll run into some white gold." Andre agreed, using his rifle as an emperor's staff.

I couldn't be as tame and theatrical so I hushed to Al's side, "where can I take a piss?"

"Use this canteen; no one lets anything drop inside or outside of them."

I felt honored to break in the piss canteen. I felt myself a parasite in the gang's honeycomb. Off I stepped into the wild fifty feet away. Slipping inside the wispy world of green galloping grass magnetized old thoughts of back home when I was a boy in the uncharted woods.

Oddly, if a fanged predator pounced on me now I would feel at peace with dying alone and free. But nothing came for me, as always. The halved-dome of the atmosphere projected towering clouds that crossed over me. A taste of thick saliva soaked my tongue and tonsils, leaking into my chest then erupted below my belt. The relief of relieving myself made the erratic joy of the woods disappear.

Back at the base Andre and Cox worked on a long grey tent with Cox spluttering frustrations to himself throwing the rods aside while cool, hard Andre slipped this into that and stood that against this with supreme ease and knowledge. Tan-man studied his GPS and began plotting our route. I sighted my scope against the furthest diametric point of our flattened circle - fifteen yards away.

"Hey, help with the tent," Andre bellowed at me as I watched Cox storm off.

Over I went. Andre pointed to my hip, "Keep your gun at reach tonight."

After we finished hammering the stakes Al breezed inside to inspect.

"We pack it back up first thing in the morning." His stance switched from Andre to me. I asked if I could go for a walk just outside the camp.

"Yes. Take this and use your phone if something happens."

"Okay."

I gently adjusted the FN Herstal into my cloth holster meant for a .1911 that was missing because I wasn't equipped with one from the start.

Ali noted it, "we have to get you a .45. Who gave you that holster?"

"I asked Andre to get me one when he went into town for our other supplies. It was when he got my boots."

He eyed my hip longer, "I think we have an extra, let me see."

He reached to un-holster his ultra-light killer. Al came back over from the luggage pile and slapped the steel in my palm: an outdated 1980's model with wood grain grip. I thanked him for adding the new compensator for relief.

Off I go! This time I took a more rushed momentum with me, rustling through the tall grass on my pulsing feet. Every heartbeat shocked my feet with booming blood. And then there was spilled blood at my boots. A grey mound of rank red, white and black was waiting in a smaller crop circle than ours. No horse flies had arrived yet, and thankfully no other predators had sniffed out delicious death either.

But the juggernaut stench of freshly hacked meat caused my balance to quiver and a ghost from my past knocked me on my ass - the old morgue stench from the frigid meat lockers of my father's work punched my head again. I only thought, before I texted Ali, I have to be away from this sight long enough to compose myself. I can't show that I'm scared ivory-white over a dead elephant!

If they found out I couldn't handle a dead elephant, post-mortem and post-autopsy, I would join this horrible heap of sin. Anchoring my nostrils inside the thin collar of my t-shirt I stood to write Ali of the discovery. All I saw was their silent bodies emerge from all sides of the circle. Genius Ali stood back and studied the body while the other three knelt to look at it. I acted strong enough to glance over the carcass with no visible queasiness.

Al told Andre to check the tracks of the perpetrators. The face had been hallowed out leaving the big dead ears of

Dumbo fluffed out at the sides. I noticed when an elephant dies it looks like a flattened parade float.

Al's long brown finger darted to the wavy sheet of skin melting into the earth, "see how they removed the tusks? It's easier to break the skull and remove the ivory than sawing or cracking it away from the face."

"You might ruin the ivory." I managed to choke out on blind instinct.

"Yes. Judging by its size it couldn't have had tusks longer than one foot. But I hate sensing the competition is close by. We'll find them and we'll get them if we spot them but that's not priority number one. Just watch out for the other poachers and the poacher hunters. We shoot first, always shoot first. He's been dead for almost twenty-four hours so we won't need to bury him or use the lime. But by morning enough animals will smell him so we'll need to leave earlier than I wanted. Come on, let's go back."

I bolted first and collected myself in the empty back room of the tent. Oddly, Ali's natural swagger around utter horror came as a comfort to my shaken senses while I coped in the corner.

His hairy paw squeezed my forearm, "we're eating dinner now. We eat together and bury our cans. Come on." When Africa is not full sunshine, storm clouds skirt the skies like a titanic UFO threatening the world.

My diabolical imagination still showed me the bloated beast oozing into a melted stain beyond the grass while we chewed in our little dinner-circle. Sometimes I despise my high-strung thoughts. I chomped my stew. We all chomped our beans.

I was relegated to the humble duty of ditch digger for our dinners. The men released their cans and plastic forks into my grey garbage bag. Al told me to bury the bag here and now. After the small grave was ready I shoveled it into the earth forever. Ali whistled a bird's exclamation from the tent and in I went.

"Did you see how they took the bull down?"

Projecting the picture onto my mind's eye I gave my best review, "yes, they hit it with a double lung shot through the right shoulder blade."

"They are competent poachers. It was a nice shot and I didn't see any trap wounds or signs of poisoning like some natives do with melons. Don't get nervous but we have enemies here hunting our ivory. Andre reported their trail beyond the elephant and we think they're moving in a group of fifteen or twenty which is tiny for a poaching gang. I guess with all the money and technology being poured into poaching now the investors don't need to hire hunting groups who hunt by the forties and fifties anymore."

I joined the others in unrolling and untying my sleeping bag and boots when Al noticed them and said I better get my rest for the night. In my corner of the tent, I imitated the men by untucking my sidearm for the night, placing it within arm's reach. My .45 Kimber slept with the safety off and one round ready in the chamber.

My imagination finally died in the dark long enough for me to sleep for four uninterrupted hours. Somewhere in the night, I heard a bird or Ali again, whistle like a lost bat beside me. And I thought only in Africa is the chirp of a bird the sound death makes.

Chapter 11

But before I rose for the day, a leaking, hum drum weariness dripped a steady drop of depression on my brain. Here I was; friendless, loveless and helpless. Hope's wheelchair creaked over the despotic sectors of my brainwork telling me this wasn't all permanent. But with the pressure of an entire continent plowing me away from all hope I could hardly believe in better things. For now, the hot new philosophy massaging my fleshy hemispheres, the two swellings of shit-pink buzzing in a case of sinew and bone, was that life moves because of time, not ambition.

My generation, being the most unfulfilled in American History, has some serious pressure points about ambition and success. We always want what's no longer available. Having to constantly avert fate and it's freshly polished guillotine, I reckoned life is nothing but timing and all ambition is futile: either what's in your fragile, unpredictable DNA allows you to get the job done or it doesn't. How many people will have a bizarre story like this to share, to claim as their own?

You don't have all of my skeleton keys jingling on your keyring, silent reader, but humor me and maybe I'll allow you to understand this world better and feel a tad closer, or a light year further, to one of our species' most colorful agents. Tucking away sorrow and fate inside the pile of these pages I cracked my knuckles and tweaked my knees for the morning marathon. I allowed Andre and Arthur to peruse the camp first in case ambush or anything death related was waiting. They quietly re-entered and I silently exited with Kimber and her tight butt jutting from my hip.

I played with the old childhood idea of masculinity with my chest poking forward and my sidearm sleeping in a hunky holster. Thankfully the dead Dumbo hadn't rotted enough to be noticed yet. Another twenty-four hours and that titanic carcass would bellow enough death sirens for half of Africa to smell. Andre and I demolished the tent and away we went.

Tan-man and Ali spotted not a spec of life with the drone that morning so the ten-mile hike started with no expectation. Thankfully the soft tissue on my feet had healed enough overnight to allow me to act more naturally than would have been possible. The titanium blue of the thunderous atmosphere leered down on us for the first seven miles then put its nightmares away for a glimpse of heaven's illusory kingdom of sauna and sky. The wet whiffs of the elephant grass shoveled H2O down our pipes and fueled an invisible urgency for us to be on the ready for anything - which in Africa, at the crack of time, is another word for mayhem.

Eventually, the adrenaline from all this scary stimulation cooled my boots and numbed my soles. Visions of my toes turning to Aloe Vera halted. When the honey-tan dream of the fibrous plains came upon us it was beautifully violent. I say this because people only visited this land of untapped suckle for blood money - always money to bring death to peace. Ali pressed his goggles to his sockets and combed long and deep.

Tan-man flew the drone into all that organic gold. The absurdity of this tiny toy zipping away into sightless areas magnified the absurdity of this by 100X. No way can a shitty human with a cheap toy invade and sack a land so imperviously ancient. But that's how it begins with us. Nature gave a simple drop of encoded blood and we painted the planet red.

And a gale of gayety struck me again – I need to explode with wild joy into a new frontier! I know now no man can resist that animal reaction to new frontiers and that's where it all goes wrong.

And in came the dreaded weather report I've waited my whole life to avoid, "Ali...we have a heard."

Al's fingers collapsed like a bridge, leaving the strap swaying the goggles around his neck as he reached for the headset, "where?"

I cynically asked from below, "yeah...where?"

"Three miles northeast. They're moving north and there are three."

"Get a better look."

For a heavenly second this hellish scene seemed to be taking place while on vacation and that second got consumed quickly.

"The bull has at least two-foot tusks. Five children and a female. Look."

Al swapped visions. "I love this thing, god!"

I tried ignoring my imagination seeing the HD close up he was having a nocturnal emission over.

"Get Tiger's men on the phone. We need to find that jeep now."

That icy rush your blood spurts into your muscles before a roller coaster ride or first virginal night with a lover came. I thought chaos and adventure were tailored for me but I had to bow out, though I was unable to now! Fuck it all!

I tried to calmly vow to myself not to shoot anything – a few heart throbbing minutes of waiting and the text came through.

"Okay, they'll drive one a mile west of here."

After the drone was zipped we hiked west for the last mile. Here in this new scene of high blue sky and squirt-sized grass Ali turned to me to say, "we'll stay clear of the Savanna arms race and those one hundred and forty clowns they have chasing the hunters and traders. This is God's country." He smiled against my dismantled grin.

His childish steps skipping to the proverbial ice cream truck continued and I wanted to kick the back of his knees in tired agitation. My bravery was steadily melting under my fidgets.

"Come on! The first of the season is the most memorable!"

I hate to concede this dark truth, but it takes someone like us who have been civilized – tried civility like a rented car only to find all too many deficiencies hidden under the hood, to know how overrated civility is. When you understand civility is an option and not a standard, the gates of the universe fly open in your face.

With the sun at our side, still sitting up in the sky during its morning stretches, the old dark woods followed alongside opposite, silent and surreal like all beginnings to bad horror stories. I tried clicking on a song in my head but my inner playlist had died. I already knew that after all of this I needed my software updated badly.

All along the spine of the brown, black and green, we paced as Ali lectured and almost lyrically prophesied on the future of his life and the world. He mentioned something about two guards guarding the jeep but when we sighted the front tires jutting from the spindly wild, four camouflaged rangers stood to watch us approach with rifles at the ready.

Ali gently flagged them down, "don't worry," he hushed from his mime's mouth, "these are our rangers. They work for Tiger."

The four glossy black rangers seemed awe-struck inside their boots when Al lent his hand to theirs. They gripped, smiled at him then to one another with jubilee surprise. In French they gifted us with the mud-toned jeep, exclaiming to it with both extended arms a 'there-it-is' pose. We all shared claws and paws and waved off. The sun was so high that the moon peeked beyond looking like a lonely holographic ostrich egg anchored in the darkest blue.

The jeep prattled and hurried like a sheep compared to Rover's roar. I knew my spot by now and tried reclining between my statues without my lower vertebrate stabbing the seat's clumsy back. Arthur snapped his drone together beside Al. Off it goes, outrunning the dirty jeep. He alerted twice, "less than a mile, keep going!"

I quickly studied Cox and Andre in their respective worlds but there's no time for scrutiny when the abyss begins churning in your eyes like the birth of a stroke with all that nasty tunnel vision. The black blobs on the crust of the horizon grew to the size and shape of one average elephant heard. I saw the young feelings of mystery and majesty defiled just like when I was a child at the bastard zoo.

Al broke one hundred feet away, causing the elephants to ignore us.

"Here's the noose." Arthur removed a black metal rod with adjustable metal ribbon attached and left the jeep.

While Ali was getting the loop sized he said to us, "this is it… Cox, Andre - be ready."

After five courteous seconds, he stomped the gas and swerved in low gear beside the family. After once around he returned, causing the brooding bull at the front to pause and eye us, facing the goofy sight of four humans in an American clown car gearing to kill him.

But Ali swooped in on the opposite side and swiped the neck of the baby calf with the noose, locking it in the customized slot originally allocated for the rear view.

Al dragged the baby a dozen yards making the heard bleat all their alarms. The baby's floppy ears, caked from a mud bath earlier, showed wet-red. Its messy tears started staining its face spotty-black. Al parked the jeep and they positioned with their rifles.

How could I not just sit there and stare? The heard scrambled. I knew Al was baiting the bull and only had to out-do it in cruelty to win. Like all hunters need to hear –

you don't hunt animals, you just kill them. A hunter is not a hunter, just a cowardly killer. If Ali hadn't taken such manly pride in the killing I may have forgiven him, honestly, but I know that's a lie too.

The baby trumpeted for help, but he only tightened the metal sling until it was weeping with a quarter of its head coming off. It was the live display of a parent's incommunicable nightmare. It bowed to the power of mortality, curling its stubby hooves under its now bloody knees. The bull lined us up, the family parting for the black ball down a slippery lane, and charged. Five or six gargantuan booms shattered my chest leaving us all breathless.

Down goes Dumbo. The gigantic rustle of the bull resigning to eternity on the short grass sounded like a cow, or ten, giving up after working on the Animal Farm all day. Al tossed an order at me, "kill the baby."

"..."

And where was the college degree or the training program, peer group or community meeting to show me how to do this properly? Arthur slapped my right arm with a comrade's encouragement. I suddenly reasoned this could be the only form of permissible murder – mercy suicide. But I still haven't forgiven myself. I aimed six inches below its young, tired and wet dying eyes. When what was left of the baby's animation ceased I shouldered my rifle back over my shocked back.

"Good, now let's get to work."

Al approached the murdered mountain. The other elephants were now stepping away in the awkward air of tragedy. The micro heap of dead infancy waved hello and danced on my head the harder I tried to block it from my sights. But piles of horror simultaneously mounted at my feet - the biggest being the blank bull biding time to be butchered. Cox and Andre knelt with newly sharpened and shined machetes slipped from black sheaths beneath the seats.

Cox hacked away while Andre took a butcher's pride in assessing the tender spots, the throw-away gristle and the big money prize at the tip of the surgeon's scalpel. After Cox had chopped around the face leaving gouges of runny red and porous white, Andre stepped in to give it the emperor's touch: gently filleting off the trunk. They left the giant grey snake on the ground then slit out the stump to release the ivory from its hard guarded face.

They snapped away like mammoth ribs being pulled apart before entering the oven. Andre handed his to Ali.

"Ah! This is a prize. Come here." Over I came.

"See the smooth ends?" He thumbed the dead nub for my displeasure. "This is what I wait for all year. I'll wrap it."

Tan-man procured a black beach towel from his drone's bag, unfolded it on the grass and gently wrapped the tusks together as one. Away they went under the seats and there I was eyeing the faded full moon in the northwest corner of the sky instead of helping them. And here I am tapping these junked keys at a third world library for every ounce of distaste to be distilled inside this little book.

When we started steaming away in Al's jeep an eclipsing sorrow began whirling inside my mind. I didn't give a damn where we were going now. Being a killer again, a killer of animals, created tiny mites of horror that began to eat away at the little peace I had left inside my terminal life.

Chapter 12

Silent reader, you don't fathom my position because my own ability with language has failed me four times before. This fifth attempt is finally taking flight after seven isolated years, but it might not stand a better chance after all. Language fails in this zone. But my old guts from old days were recycling old brawn as fuel to keep going. Eager ethnic teenagers study diligently at the public computers here and I'm still heaving from the struggle to scrawl the events of the previous chapter.

I cannot believe I am me.

I'll let these growing brown people accelerate towards their suffocating ambitions while I continue to compartmentalize my own with transcribing this novel. They'll turn to rum heads long before any individual ambition is realized and rewarded. Now this silly young dreamer and his wounded ambitions from old days of unjust pains continue writing inside his new home – the world at large.

Arthur had let the drone's ghost line out all the way until he nearly lost signal, "I need to bring it back; it's going in and out."

Ali parked the jeep while Arthur contorted the controls ten feet away.

"How long will it take to bring it back?" Ali reclined his seat and kicked his ruffled legs across the wheel, "ten or fifteen minutes."

This was the waiting period I recalled at the dentist's office between root canals when I could afford a dentist. Cox hopped off and sat on the earth for a smoke in the sun. Andre sat like a master's watchful Doberman, scanning the scene ahead with his flat brain waves. Cox's Camels swarmed up my nose leaving my sinus canals stuffed.

"You okay?" Ali cranked his neck to me.

"Yeah, I'm just having some weird allergies."

"I get them too." As his beard chomped out cool words they mingled with the smoke and rode the wind together. "I would normally get mad but it's the start of the new season and the drone we got needs to be tested like a new car so I'm not upset," he nudged Arthur's shoulder, "if Arthur plays a little too." Along the multi-grain plain lay the centimeter-thin smudge of forest.

I noted Al kept eyeing it and fidgeting with his thumbnails as thoughts ruined his rest. After enough dirt was extracted he poked one clean thumb to the distant growth, "going through the jungle at night is like playing in the boogeyman's basement - you'll see."

And the boogeyman waited, letting his brow and beard sag with sweat.

"When nature runs a fever like this it's trying to get us to leave like germs from its blood." Al picked more nails, edging out and flicking the flakes of debris, "if I were a germ

I'd live in blood too: surfing from one hot plate to another, always swimming and always mating."

He re-junked his nails by raking out the stray particles in his beard like the teeth in a cotton gin. "These days if you love somebody don't expect anything in return. Reciprocation is a charade today. We're all animals anyway and that's the fun of it all: chasing and mating."

I tried adding my sentiments to his talk, "sometimes I think of how short life really is and I want to scream and cry that I didn't get to love everyone on the planet; ugly, old, skinny, fat, rich, poor, healthy, crippled. I want to love everyone but you can only truly love a few people in life."

After more beard-scratching, Cox flicked his cigarette sideways after suffocating its butt on his black boot. Rising, he slunk down a very steep slope hidden in the folds and contours of the grass. Ali snapped his thumb and index finger accompanied by a 'hey' for me to take Cox's spot. I splayed my legs on the grass and leaned back.

Al began in a chummy tone, "Cox is angry. Find out what happened between him and Andre yesterday and tell me. I need to say the right thing. Cox isn't allowed to drink on the hunt so I'm not sure if it's that or,"

"I'll take care of it."

"Don't take care of anything other than what I said."

"I'll find out, that's it."

Breezing over, I caught Cox mid-zip as he finished draining his thankful bladder. "Eh."

"Eh."

I unfolded and slipped away the paper from a gum slice and stuck it in my teeth and handed one to his palm, "so, what's up with you and Andre?"

Unhanding the gum to one dank pocket he extracted a green Bic lighter and snapped sparks from its dry mouth until he chucked it.

"Niggers don't know how good they had it when they were slaves – at least they worked."

"Hey…"

"No, I don't take orders from a black bastard like that."

I entered parent mode, "why do you call him that?"

"Because they don't have Shakespeare, they don't have Beethoven." I, of course, would normally beg to disagree but with a lousy souse like this who knows how he can interoperate the truth?

"They still live here and act the same as they did a thousand years ago but in our clothes."

This nonsense couldn't continue. Feeling his tirade wobble under the duress of damaged lungs I broke in, "what about all of the cities here and all of the advancements? What about all of the black Shakespeares here and abroad?"

"Are you kidding me? Do you think they would have any of it without us? They couldn't even stop bloody American farmers from keeping them like chickens in a cage like that fucker should be."

I despise myself, or a certain energy I advertise, for only attracting sad people.

I toned down my tone and humbly defended my home and this one too, "for a long time blacks never had to say anything about their position in America to whites because they always knew white people were wrong."

"You're a pussy, man. You use stress balls and I use a gun to handle shit. Murder is so much more replenishing than a stress ball. If art and philosophy could save the world it would have. I don't need to hear a bullshit poet tell me about what I do."

"How come you hate him so badly?"

"Does he smile?" This sluggish retort left my brows erect and my hands palm-up. "No, what's his fucking problem?"

"You don't smile."

"But at least I treat everyone else with respect!"

"You're homesick, like me a little."

"Yeh..."

The Camel smoldering down his throat worked its wonder for his nicotine starved nerves. He smoked against the sun and it showed rising vapors just above his shadow. I reasoned through a colorful fog that I didn't need to persuade him. His unjust and unruly logic couldn't justify breathing let alone a racist beef. Losing my balance I fought to stride back to Ali with a jumbled report. Arthur still stood watching his visuals and I passed his breathing body to slump beside his boss.

"What happened?"

"He wouldn't tell. He hates all black people and is fed up with Andre over him giving orders and not being friendly enough or something. He's in a bad way."

Al tapped the wheel with all ten digits in order then in reverse, "well, it's strange of us to think everything white is beautiful. I suspect if ivory were black it wouldn't be desired as much. It's odd. He never let out that side of himself before, but it doesn't surprise me."

"I think he's a racist drunk."

"Andre is far more valuable than him but he's still very important. We need a good, competent shot out here. Maybe you can take his place in the future? Of course, he has problems with addiction and I've warned him only once about it interfering with his work."

"The term addict is now used by villains who act like victims."

"Well…most people aren't worth saving just like most people aren't worth fucking."

"Ha!"

"We do not need therapy, we need honesty."

"You should be a writer."

"Like you? I wouldn't know where to begin. I wouldn't want any publicity of me getting out there, now with this and my past."

"I feel the same way at times."

And that sad silence that separates lives took over. I saw at that moment that all the relationships we ever had with others had hit rock bottom. Time had flooded the quarries all of our old relationships moldered in and we were never waiting again for new ones. We were done with old affections. Tan-man suddenly slipped in, "we can get ready now."

As Arthur stood anticipating his pet Ali hit me with a cryptic quip, "you know you were always meant to be here with me and the rest of us. You had no say in it."

He waited for my words in the wind, "I guess I must be blessed."

"It's better than thinking you're damned."

"I'll remember that line."

"Use it for your book."

"I will, maybe near the end."

My jagged k9s matched his gangly killer's row with the grim reaper peeping in the middle. A wise wink from one eye and he watched the guided drone fly home. The others clambered back to the jeep. Cox and Andre settled on either side of me as Tan-man disassembled his pet.

Deciphering what Arthur blurted to Ali I unscrambled something about the drone not spotting any elephants but instead groups of poachers, scientists or adventures. With all the wind pounding my head along the drive I couldn't understand most of it. This is where I began to learn that it can take days to find those elusive white missiles strutting around this land.

Over the three month hunt, we spent more than half of it chasing ghosts, hunches, feelings, and predictions inside Africa's ether-like air. Preparing to slit my inner child's throat for this deathly long haul, I began figuring out how to bring the rest of my novel to life if I survived.

Chapter 13

Taking a fourth of the day for the drone to canvas twenty miles inside a space of one thousand miles was obviously less than productive unless luck and timing interceded in our favor. An arrangement was made with Tiger's men later that fruitless evening when certain neon sprouts and florescent flower bulbs began charming the floor of the park nestled in Congo. After he got off the phone, just before the sun slept, Ali called us together like lost ducks.

"A few of Tiger's men are positioned on the outside of the park. Tomorrow we will get another drone and more fuel. They haven't spotted anything yet but they're on the lookout too."

Cox sat back and warmed the front of a cigarette. The turquoise and magenta skewed horizon was morphing into an ebony blanket slowly rising to shroud the earth. This novel was put on indefinite hold until an appropriate situation sprang up for me to run away and write.

We made an immature fire in a heel-dug pit. Andre volunteered to stand guard as postman and once the world was drowned in darkness two red eyes showed when he activated one of the three pairs of night vision goggles. Cox chugged Camel after Camel, eyeing Andre's pulsing silhouette beyond the fire. Every drag caused his skeletal face to glow lava-orange in the dark.

We had weapons barrel-up at our sides as we munched canned oranges, more slimy beans and exotic bread that sanded my throat.

"They'll bring more food too. I knew choosing a jeep this season would be more fun."

"Excuse me Ali, but I believe the word is funner. I know you would want to know the correct pronunciation."

He noted it, "Funner – I'll remember now."

The others let the fire beguile their primal attention. But I know the tricks flames play in the night when a day is dead and night seems like a new adventure. The ghost stories all of us could perpetuate around this fire on this night enticed me for a millisecond before Cox slammed his can into the pit, flaring a low storm of sparks and molten shrapnel.

"This fucking nigger slaps me and he just walks around getting away with it."

Andre stepped forward behind Al from the blind background, arms folded and flexed. Cox flicked a final cigarette into the scattered fire before pushing himself up to walk away.

Ali's calm anchored voice grabbed Cox by his heels.

"Hey. I only tell people once – it's over now."

And the implication sucked his manhood dry, leaving it denuded and barely alive like ectoplasm in Al's back pocket. Cox raised his first two fingers, giving Andre a V-sign off into the night, walking his problematic path. Andre's arms rose with his long and serious inhale while the reflection of coal and flames rippled his torso. No lone Camel bud burned out there so eyeing him was frivolous. Al, now circled by us other three, smelled then sipped his canteen.

"Hey," he passed me the water, "when this is over we always have two celebrations – one at the spot of the final hunt and the other with the purchaser wherever he lives: this season it's Tiger in China. Last season and the seasons before are all colorful chapters in life."

Giving a thumbs-up I licked the running drop on my chin. Andre's cheeks creased at the memory of the seasons and their endings.

"We made a good move this season by signing with Tiger. He's very professional and has more connections than any other purchaser I've dealt with. When I first started out, how many years again? I made so many dumb compromises with the purchasers."

"Ali, it's purchaseers, I'm only trying to help."

"Purchaseers. Thank you."

He finished the canteen, "I made my first big paycheck by riding horseback through the Savanah with gun runners who stole half the shipment before we finished the hunt. It was all a big fuck up. I went to a port in Kismayo to sell what tusks I had left when the gang split and I found there on that old dock what I wanted for the rest of my work days."

His emulation of American English touched not my romanticism but my innate parental pity. I falsely encouraged now just to see the gorgeous sight of him fall for me in the worst way. He rebuilt the flames with his boots, kicking the hot refuse together again like Humpty Dumpty's fireball brother.

"It has been a mountain chase since then. And I'm on my fifth mountain."

I bolted in, "that's a lot of ivory!"

Andre farted after my excited crack causing a reaction of clockwise chuckling. Under my giggling mask, I allowed myself to really enjoy this dumb gesture inside our boys' clubhouse. Arthur politely handed Andre an empty bean can then Andre flung it to me to dispose of in the peeled plastic bag.

Al started again, "yeah...I've been in the oddest situations all my life."

"Ali, I can totally empathize."

Sighting my junior sincerity he agreed without words. Andre farted three more times before laughing himself back into the dark. Arthur shot out wisecracks and we heard Andre guffaw in the dark. After, his electric red eyes vanished.

"Like I said, this business is wonderful if you can appreciate good hunting and good fun and really good money."

The pile of accumulated bones in Al's elephant graveyard was becoming unearthed by my anger's invisible hands. My anarchic side bullied its way through my better senses and forced me to begin tickling Ali with jabs about his morals and conscience.

"Have you ever felt any feelings about the elephants you murder?"

His dry reddish tongue felt for his false tooth on the bull's eye. It rubbed and caressed the tooth until his viper's smirk grew to a smile, finally evolving into a single word reply, "never…"

"So it's all business for you."

"Business and pleasure, remember?"

"Hunting is fun but isn't a good death better than just a plain old murder? I mean isn't murder and tired old death cliché at this point in history?"

"How do you mean?"

"A good death is an artful death. A bad death is an artless death."

"I forgot we have an artist here. Tell me what an artful death is, it might be different than my definition."

"An artful death is an original one. It's a new way to murder and for an original purpose. An artless death is a clichéd death, something passé and contemptible for the sole reason of being bland. An artful death should mirror high art – it should be original and completely indicative of the individual. No one can replicate its genius."

"Well," the men brushed around at my sly rebuke, passing the canteen and checking themselves for certain stains, "I've killed in ways you might not have thought of. I assume you've only killed animals?"

"Of course." Somewhere behind the night's black curtain, I heard Andre's steps approach to eavesdrop on the new engaging talk.

"So let's stay in your world. How have you killed your animals?"

"With guns."

"That doesn't sound very artful."

"Ali, I'm not accusing you of not being original or creative. I just want to know your most interesting methods."

His thumbs picked and flicked random debris off his wrinkled cargo pants.

"I've used everything from poison arrows to poisoned fruit to kill elephants. I learned those ways from the villagers who can't afford guns or ammunition so they build traps and use natural ways. Where you come from no one needs to be so unique or imaginative with how they hunt or kill."

I rustled enough nerves in his skin but I wanted to mutilate his sciatica without being pinned for mayhem.

"How does it make you feel knowing you're causing so many tears, so much bloodshed and pain throughout all of nature and greater humanity just for something as ordinary as money?"

He showed a grim glare that pierced me until his rebuttal arrived in a slow, measured tone, "it's not *you* are, it's *we* are."

"Sorry - *we*. I know how it makes *me* feel but how about *you*?"

He unscrewed the screeching lid of the canteen off and on, eventually finding contained air.

"No. How about you? How's that novel coming?"

His words carried a dreary undertone of implied warning.

"Tell me about literature and why it's so essential for you to keep writing even though you're doing no one any good?"

My brain sprawled for the lightning witticism, "I guess it's the challenge. There's no cheat code for literature. It's the art that mirrors life most. You cannot have a secret talent, like a dopey savant outplaying Beethoven, which unlocks the magic of good literature."

As he leaned forward his left hand felt back for something as I continued to break the tension with a satisfactory answer.

"Literature is in trouble because novels are too preachy to be absorbed now by all these armchair preachers."

"Yeah…"

His Herstal came to the end of my nose, the barrel plunging the pale grease strings from my pores as he pressed.

"I've read your novel so far and I don't like what you say about me. In fact, I don't like anything you say you sneaky American ass. Tell me if this is an artful death…"

His thumb slowly rested the hammer on the primer.

"Ha!" With one swipe he wiped my brow with the barrel.

"You would have died like a soldier! Come on, you're not afraid of a little death, are you? I trust my partners and friends more than that. Do you think I care what you write?!"

The others jabbered nonsense as my milk-white skin and ice-soaked blood flushed itself like a new toilet.

"Come on! I'm playing…"

"You know why I didn't react?"

"Why?"

His encouraging tone stayed as he re-holstered the Herstal.

"My father used to put me in spots like that."

"With a gun?!"

"Never with a gun, but with other things in other ways." "Hey! How many people were killed in your hometown last year?"

"It's an average of five to six hundred a year. Between the two worst cities there are almost fifteen hundred murders annually and that's not including rapes, robberies, assaults, vandalism and every other crime. People die and suffer in every way irony and tragedy can conceive of back home and I was in it my whole life. I should be in prison given what I've done but back home in my city you can get away with, uh, stuff over and over and over again."

"Sounds like home for all of us." The others nodded in their secret memories, remembering again that there really is no justice. Once you learn the big secret that there's no such thing as justice, you can understand so much more. And when you see that understanding in someone else, no matter countries, languages, religions etc. you see that being included in the hidden brotherhood of horror is just as liberating and mesmerizing as any ecstasy around.

Papa Al let out a maddening simile to the splash of stars above, "I bet the universe is a lot like the ocean – there's a lot of mystery there but it's all disappointing."

He gave a long smooch to the swerving clouds. I ripped the canteen from the sand only to find what Ali found – contained air. Once the enormity of all that disappointment beyond the clouds spanked our asses we quieted.

A slack-jawed Al had the twinkling of the sparkling sky dancing on his funny tooth. He soaked it with his messy taste buds before sucking the flavor back down.

"I had this tooth made from the first elephant I ever killed. We were removing its face when I got sentimental and chipped a piece of its tusk with my knife and pocketed it."

"Did you know what you wanted to do with it when you shaved it?"

"No. The most satisfying part of getting a tooth carved from ivory is the fleshy smell and taste it drips down your throat and up your nose. I've grown to love it. And it never goes away – that was very unexpected."

"The weirdest thing about humans, to me, is we can't keep flesh out of our mouths."

"True."

He swapped the bone-dry canteen for one with warm stale water waiting.

"Ah, we can't keep liquids out either."

His serious boots came alive when he brushed asphalt-black dirt onto the rest of the fighting flames.

"Let's sleep. I don't know if you know how long an endurance test this hunt will be. The travel alone is too much for almost anybody."

He deployed a teaser itinerary for tomorrow by calling out a mental list: "meet Tiger's men, map more of the area – maybe go to another area, eat and drink and sleep and hopefully kill. We'll have gone over most of Africa and some of China by the time this is over. But what happens in between rests on luck and timing along this three month timeline."

I corked the talk, "well, I knew before I left home I was signing up for a vacation."

"I thought your little pamphlet said adventure?"

I was at a loss.

"How did you read my pamphlet?"

I watched the men leave for the tent. I was the last to go to bed.

*****

Destroying the evidence of our pre-dawn presence allowed me to catalog my feelings about murdering an animal again. This burden, this situation, had given me a sneak peek of my future-self living with a ghastly albatross around my neck for the remainder of life. But all of that projecting did me no good and I tucked it away with the other soiled linens in my dungeon's dirty hamper for later rummaging.

A manly job was before me again and my rumination got me in a jam that would lead me to the great blackout sooner than I wanted. My infant novel was beginning to whine and kick for some due attention. Yes! I really am a writer and my baby needs feeding – at our next camp, I will write furiously.

We proceeded in the jeep across the wavy plains of the Congo and into the sight of five very serious, very clean Asians wrangling a bull elephant away from its life. Ali broke so hard it pulled us forward and jerked us back.

"Hey! Stop!"

He fired Herstal into the clouds five times before they, not the bull, broke their act to gaze at us five.

He ordered in Chinese over the bull's pawing and groaning. Dumbo plopped on his ass while the men argued back with Ali until he screamed, "Ali!" All but Dumbo hushed and paused. Two backed away as the others jumped to their feet for business. As Al marched to them, the four of us inspected the elephant tied between the triangle of jeeps. Seeing the dozen or so wounds along its belly and back showed a bungled poach.

Cox was the first to judge, "amateurs." The sight made my stomach mix tears and vomit inside itself and forced me to see Ali. Tiger's militarized men had run into the bull, or the bull had crossed them, as they waited en route for us. They pointed and showed air-guns and air-walking, with two fingers for them and four for the elephant, illustrating what was obviously lost in translation.

Abruptly one of Tiger's men took a ten gauge shotgun and erupted it into the elephant's face, leaving it to collapse with a thousand craters in its face. Ali un-holstered Herstal and fired between the man's eyes. Tiger's men retracted from their dead comrade. He barked to me in English if the ivory is ruined in any way the others will die too.

"Get your rifle on them."

Unslinging my .458 I pointed the magnum at their tight cluster from my waist. The kick from this bastard would be enough to pulsate them to the floor even if I missed. The movements from the far corner of my right eye I assumed to be Cox and Andre knifing the tusks from the impotent jaw of the elephant. I was frozen into tough-guy mode and could not afford to seem silly with checking on the work of my comrades.

Tiger's men held their hands high. My appendages ran sweat-warm and fever-cold. The suicidal thought of passing out or going limp could not enter so I didn't let it.

"Hey!"

Al called for me to join, so in my stick 'em up position I motioned for them to follow first. My little impromptu signal of telling two elephant poachers to vamoose this way with my rifle made me feel real to myself.

Hell yes, I exist and these men know it. They believe the body that is me and the long and heavy weapon I wield. Their zombie candor moved over to Al while I courageously pointed the gun at their backs. Cox checked the moon-colored sabers and found no chinks in their frames – only the hairline fractures of nature's natural wear and tear.

"They are good."

"Good."

The two laughable losers had the gall to point to the tusks and then to themselves. Al tried to untangle their meaning but he huffed a bemused exclamation, "I guess I shot their only interpreter!"

Tan-man, the terribly talented and thoughtful among us, apparently knew more stray Chinese than Ali and provided the bridge, "They want the tusks."

"Ask them if they have our goods." Arthur began the pantomime, probing with this gesture and that word. The two worked out their story with Arthur guiding it in for us.

"Ah, yes. They have it in one of their cars."

"Give me the phone."

My left hand, pillaring the wood stock of Mr. Magnum, started sweating and slightly slipping forward. But I was as stiff as Andre surveying the skyline. I almost asked him 'hey, let's swap. I'll take five.' But this demanded more of a serious back-home work ethic.

"Okay, thank you, Tiger. Here." Ali handed them the satellite phone.

The talker agreed and bowed to his boss's orders. He gave the phone back to Al and he spoke to Tiger again. Hanging up, really beeping away, Ali quietly reached for Cox's P-90 and gently sprayed the two across their torsos. The P-90 sounded like an automatic airsoft gun with rapid pops instead of the concussive booms of our rifles and side arms. Their low moans and serious whimpers, almost dying with the agony we're born with, floated on the grass as their bodies wormed for relief.

"He said to kill them they're so incompetent."

"I think he meant incontinent."

"Whatever. Help get the tusks into the truck and I'll grab our new supplies." Shouldering my gun I took the tip of one tusk and slid it down my palm, just below the bloody base. I somberly carried it to the jeep and tucked it beneath the back seat with its twin that Andre carried. Death now stung me from all angles.

From the poacher's SUV Arthur and Ali fetched a new drone, a case of bottled water, packaged and canned foods, and the guns, ammunition, and wallets of the five. They couldn't really be identified if there wasn't an audience, I mean evidence. Al kept their paper currency and chucked the creased leather bats into the plastic bag meant for tonight's trash.

I survived again. The confidence I got from weathering another gauntlet made me feel that I had finally found a job I could keep, but I didn't know for how long. Again, I don't shove my luck down anyone's throat let alone my own. Let me keep living moment to moment and see what happens.

Chapter 14

Life is a story that writes itself. All I had to do was record our progression of snipping and snatching tusks, which quickly included the trade of the jeep for a big new all-terrain SUV even more eager and lovable than old Rover. The procession of rotting elephant bones lay in a miles-long zig-zag behind. Counting after the first month we had left thirty-five to forty bodies behind us.

Andre and Ali took box cutters to the floorboard and lowered a pine crate stenciled 'SPICES' in five languages. They packed the dry ivory with chili peppers and sawdust – provided by a transporter of Tiger's. When we had a burgeoning supply of elephant fangs rattling inside under us, one of the transporters would take it to the designated holding site. Ali said when we ship this off from the port, if we're stopped, the sniff-dogs won't catch the scent of the ivory suffocating under the bold herbs and undead wood.

At the beginning of our second month, we slipped to a clearing in Congo that housed a helipad with chopper waiting. The same pilot that flew us in last month on the private jet saluted our unmarked vehicle as we wheeled up. The crate was carted by all of us onto the black jet ranger with built-in .50 caliber turrets. We loaded what was nearly a million dollars in death. And my nerves at this juncture were flexed like a king jellyfish about to whip his one-hundredth intrusive victim invading his territory.

The aches and pains of the unyielding and ever mounting hunt showed themselves in the form of a tender lower back, yawning hips, crying kneecaps, insomnia eyes and unchecked hair. Anytime a river or lake was approached we bathed in the ruddy warmth of their natural waters. These excursions substituted showering for the three months.

"We can't risk the shipment by going anywhere civilized."

Ali informed after a dumb question from me. Most nights we sat huddled and zapped around the whistling fire, eating our pre-cooked salt-infused foods without a word or gesture. As the writer, I naturally stepped into my observant role whose position never faltered from the bottom of the totem. At the start of the second month, Ali sent Cox to bed without dinner because he mouthed off to me about being an incompetent waste.

Apparently, my bullets were always lost, the sight never fixed properly, the bolt jamming and the fat slug always missing its mark. But papa Ali kept me in his concerned arms, hoping the gun would come back to life and my aim restored. But no such luck. All I could do was lend a helping hand or two. My bag and its treats treated me nightly with the relief of writing.

"I hope you can write in the dark." Al snapped when I asked for a lantern.

"I'll try."

And I got pretty decent at sketching my memories blindly. After a week into the second month, when my beard became bulletproof shag weaved to my face, Tan-man and Ali flew two drones out. In the first month, we traversed a quarter of Congo, even with our relentless marches and ceaseless driving it felt like we traveled the world five times over while leaving legions of corpses behind our tornado's path.

"There's a group ten miles northeast travailing in our direction. They're on foot, toting rifles and machine guns in army fatigues."

Tan-man quietly conspired with Al, "are they Boko Haram or Janjaweed?"

"No, just park rangers looking for hunters. They look better this year but they don't see us because like dogs they're too incompetent to look up. We'll go west after tonight. They're in jeeps with four to a car."

For the past week, I'd noted Andre poking Cox with this move or that word. Andre had let enough of his professionalism slip with the labor of living through the hunt to trip Cox here and jar him there. What caused this new scuffle was Andre, winking to me before taking his sidearm and shooting up the grass at Cox's boots claiming when Cox was in breathless hysterics that there was a snake ready to bite.

Cox fired two rounds two inches above Andre's dome. That was the only window where anyone saw Andre flinch with fear. Ali jumped passed me to untangle Andre's clenched forearms from Cox's narrowing neck. This was the only time I thought one of my comrades might be killed. And Al, after two French cries, penetrated Andre's pride into releasing Cox. Al pointed one finger for them both, "next time will be the last time."

Tan-man, oblivious to this playground scuffle, calmly told Al we could go another two or three miles into the hills before we risk facing the rangers. And when the drones flew home we pulled away with the dusk at our wheels. I despaired being the human wedge on the back seat dividing the two unruly gents. The burning in both men for blood slithered through me into each other.

Their game had hit a peak and when the next one lost it would be for keeps. And here I am – always being victimized in some way. Between the brutes, I bravely bit a red gum stick I found lodged in one corner of my bag.

And when the world didn't break to stardust at my chewing I sat stiffly in my sleepy solitude. My minds arms rock me to sleep in all stupid scenarios where my iconic artist's front is threatened. And everyone buys it. Even if they don't, they act like they do.

I even had guts enough to try blowing and biting microbubbles from a brand that doesn't pop when you blow. I must have seemed like an exotic fox munching bubble wrap in the face of death. Cox curled up at the window when he felt me recline. Andre's profile primed the world for his coming presence whenever he looked out the window. His veins and arteries sprouted on his hands, arms, and head but his breathing was still mummified.

Nothing really added up when you did the math. Nothing ever fully does. Everyone needs to make room for leftovers or the big mysteries we call undiscovered science. Magic is science. Time is wisdom. That's why the universe is so much smarter than we are. That's why at times I felt a blabbering baby at my best inside Africa, on this antique rock of life.

Ali had gone the extra light year to shroud me under his wing to keep me nurtured and protected. His mother-hen actions made my clumsiness and mishaps scratch-proof to the arrows being lobbed from the eyes of Cox and Tan-man. All I had to do was be this version of me and I won all the approval of this world.

I can never forget that there is great strength in weakness and great wisdom in ignorance. Ali and I are proof of the success caused by curling the rule book with blackening flames. Running down elephant herds, wasting whole families, had gotten so mechanical and passé that when we approached them, like now, all I thought was 'back to work...'

*****

Al had the grotesque genius of hooking up a small plug-in skillet to the outlet beside the radio to secretly simmer dinner for us. It was hunks of the latest bull we eradicated with slugs that slept dead beside the vehicle. We surgically removed the face and wiggled and cracked the ivory away earlier. We had a quick rendezvous with one of Tiger's agents for the skillet, among other supplies.

Through the steaming glass, we watched Ali from outside the SUV fry the elephant flesh in low-grade olive oil with our only metal utensil – one seven inch bowie knife nestled to Al's green belt. The idea worked in keeping the ghastly scent vexing around inside the now forever tainted interior. He waved 'hello' as a dead mist came alive to consume him.

Andre's steak was done first and Al wiped away the condensation of the skin's tears and waved him in. "Quickly!" he warned. He hopped in to eat and leave without too much of the smell escaping. Surrounding the car we examined Andre gobble the skin cake and exit the vehicle.

I explored the routes of excuses for my not participating in the crime. The anvil-whiff slammed my gut and caused me to bolt backward towards the tent to prepare for my night of writing and scheming. After fifteen minutes of watching the tent's vinyl bleed the fading orange of the sun's surrender, Cox stumbled in with his usual detached walk of the typical night stalker. His gait was always disjointed and wobbly resembling a drunken octopus's walk on the shore.

"It tastes like hell."

"Then why are you sucking what's left off of your teeth and down your throat?"

"Fuck off."

"Okay."

He reached down and scrambled my papers, fetching a crumpled page to inspect.

"Nah, this is no good. Don't write about yourself or this place. No one will read this anyway. Put some dragons, wizards or vampires in it. Maybe you'll get famous then and quit trying to run with us."

My tarnished page found a bull's eye at my feet as he let it flutter down.

"I'm surprised you can read because you can hardly talk. What do you know about writing?"

"That you can't do it."

He tried a bold but lazy intimidation with his stance and tone but I only picked up my paper and slid it back in with its numerical family.

"You can't take anything out on Andre so you pick on me." "He's not useless. I can't believe Ali hasn't given you one warning yet. If I were him I would have left your incompetent ass behind with the other elephants. This is my last year in this business if fuckers like you are joining up. This can't go on much more if cunts like you are getting in it. I can't stand amateurs."

Arthur came in the tent, "he wants you now."

Packing and zipping this novel in my duffle, I approached the stinking vehicle with tensity for not having a ready-made excuse to not eat. Cox spoiled my planning of a lie. Al waved me inside.

In the sauna of burning skin and blood, I politely crossed my hands and urged the paper plate away, "keep it for yourself. I'm not really in the mood to eat. I just got done writing."

"You sure?"

"Yes, go ahead. If anyone deserves seconds it's you."

Breathing, measuredly, through my teeth and not my nose he gladly began sucking and chewing.

I went for the handle, "Wait."

Head hung in his lap with a mouth full of misery he wagged an index finger at me. "Let me finish before you open the door."

Thankfully the freak ate like a duck. He used a whole can of bathroom deodorizer inside before we hauled out.

Tan-man was waiting for us to exit, "The Rangers are just two miles away now. They've settled for the night but we're taking a risk being here."

Al considered the rising moon. It was about to shine any minute.

"We'll have Cox stand guard tonight."

Thank you, papa Ali!

"When will he sleep?"

"Tomorrow night. He deserves to do some extra work anyway."

Thankfully a stream of rocky grey clouds erased the moon, using it as a blindfold to camouflage us for the night. Cox couldn't lash out when Ali told him his duty for the night. Through the partially undone window of the tent, I saw Cox slap the coals out with one boot. The open screen would have allowed me to sleep all night if I had only stopped thinking a string of silent rangers might approach from the woods.

By 2 AM, in the preternatural silence, our breaths fumed a fishy atmosphere. And I awoke sometime in the middle of our collective slumber to the silence of Cox: no smoke, no grumbles, and no movement. And in the morning, around six, his head stood on its neck showing his expression the moment before decapitation: drunken features still begging to sleep. His broken windpipe and unevenly cut skin skirted the cold ashes of the pit. Andre said he never looked better.

*****

"He died being himself."

"How did it happen?"

"No, he still looks stupid."

Andre positioned beside the low head and dimmed his eyes and hung his open mouth into a drunk's agonized frown.

"Go check the tracks, see who came in. Andre sprung up from his crouch and began the serious inspection.

Ali was heating a tin mug of water for a scoop of instant Kaffee. I leashed myself to his side.

I needed papa's protection now.

"I guess if there was a ranger who played cowboy under the moon he could have done it. There better be tracks or another head will roll." With the brown sack of aromatic crystals in hand, he punted Cox away.

When Al got into an introspective and contemplative mood a barrier of seclusion surrounded him. Ali assessed the pieces like a chess wizard before his hand reached for any action. He whistled to Tan-man and whispered for them to send out the drones. Up and away!

Al and Arthur stood side by side slyly sharing thoughts and predictions plus the occasional theory. Now the Rangers were four miles north of us and as Ali said he just knew it was them who snuck in while we snored: all intuition and experience. Andre trekked in from the elephant grass with his report. A well-trodden, almost stomped down, path of a careless Ranger was seen in the grass and disappeared to nowhere.

"How does their path end in the grass? They came from somewhere."

Andre could only shake his head. The long dueling grass blades on either side of the path dared us to solve the mystery or hike away without ever knowing. That vacant trail that lead to Cox's death could have been from an animal or a Ranger but it kept sniggering at us the longer we watched its silent answers scream over our fixed heads.

"Today we travel, we'll gather the tent and leave. They can have the rest of him."

As Andre and I rolled the tent I cracked, "this is easier for both of us now."

And for a flash I envisioned Andre swiping off the head with one quick machete slice in the dark. We retracted inside our silent camaraderie and pulled together for a two hundred mile drive east. On the third silent hour, with windows locked and drones asleep, an offensive musk piped through the air vents and made us rotate to search for the unburied treasure of dead jewels.

A melted fragment of flattened parade floats lay smeared along a dirt path leading to some Bruno-esque village a few miles away. Apparently, the natives had poisoned these elephants with tainted arrows dipped in toxins. Four adults lay smudged on the dirt.

"Look."

Al pointed to specific areas of the mushed bodies.

"Look at this. I've heard this was starting to happen but I hadn't seen it until now."

The genitals and nipples had been cut away. Tan-man asked out loud as his scrutiny recoiled away from it, "why do they do this now?"

"I don't know."

Horse flies had long begun eating the rotting bodies and breeding, leaving their baby maggots to mature inside the blackened orifices. As a far off microwave, the sun had been overcooking it for weeks. Mother Nature sure knows what she's doing in the kitchen! We drove off. Everything was thought, not said, until we parked and unpacked for our new plight that night.

Chapter 15

"If the Rangers are tracking us we'll need more surveillance. I won't lose another man to them."

Ali jabbered on his satellite phone to Tiger in a conference call with his disfigured business buddy. I pictured that Chinese penguin squawking behind his finely crafted desk believing he was leasing nature herself with his fat undercover deals. A personality like that exists and I still cannot believe I've encountered it twice now.

After Al beeped off he called this week's messenger to name the roll call of items; disposable toiletries, cold medicine for the men's congestion and exhaustion, more water, new boots for Arthur, a new tire for the vehicle and more maps in case the two laptops with portable satellites collapsed again. The next pick-up site was just inside the Ituri jungle. The Ituri Forest's borders dissolved beside our wheels and all Al did was nick the power steering right and in we went.

Apparently, old Russian gunrunners had already made rude paths and bitchy trails in the area so we re-used them.

"Hey, the Pygmy's are really easy to cheat. They call them Bambenga here and shopkeepers and general middlemen run in and out of the forest with gold, wild meat, and timber. So if you see some and they have stuff you want just give them some change or a fingernail and they'll forfeit their estate. A lot of people here eat the Pygmies so don't feel too bad about it. They're so inbred and tiny but have such a tight culture and techniques that some tribes eat them and believe they'll absorb their hunting powers and eyesight. I had an old scrapbook of war pictures and in it, a Mayi-Mayi Chief paraded around the village with a dried Pygmy infant around his neck. I lost that book somewhere."

"At least I have mine."

"Yeah…"

Four tattered natives coasted down the muddy red road on bicycles with fastened sacks and copious naps on their seats.

"These are Toleka traders. If you think we have it bad they're going about two hundred miles to deliver their stuff on this road today."

"How far are we going in?"

"A few miles. If they approach us they're harmless. I've only dealt with them a few times. I'll get us some treats like black rainforest honey."

"Do they make music or any kind of art?"

"All I know is one Pygmy tribe called the Mbuti has a funeral song for their dead: 'There is darkness upon us; darkness all around, there is no light. But it is the darkness of the forest, so if it really must be, even the darkness is good.'"

"I really like that. They're obviously not dim when it comes to life and death."

A creature like a zebra stood deathly still like a museum piece of the past beside our windows. Al gave the tour guide's commentary again, "that's an Okapi. They only exist here."

"They look like the unicorns of Africa."

"So much war has gone on here but you wouldn't know it. You'll see lots of unmarked graves filled with little girls who were sex slaves for the latest warlord who tried stealing this land. The military camps where they were taken just dumped their bodies back home, here in the jungle."

"This jungle is so disarming though, it's ironic."

"Even your unicorn will gorge you on the wrong day. Rainbows and gold are usually traps and deceptions."

"I guess the people here, once you get so tough it just rots your mind. All you can be is tough."

"Imagine those kids back in Bruno. Think of how good they have it compared to the Pygmies." For the time being, I had walled the memory of Bruno up.

BAM! Out goes the tired tire.

Al's rusted hand punched the steering wheel's eye and sounded the happy honk of the horn. Immediately Arthur's fingers began dialing Tiger's number. Tiger's men were baited behind one mile away inside brush the size of greater Brazil. Al's exasperated snarls were common now when dealing with the low-rent dregs.

Arthur hung up, "They'll be here in ten minutes."

"Coming up that road?"

"Of course…"

Reading about the heaving walls of vault-tight foliage and vegetation from other authors is one thing but having a first-person vantage of this hulking organic high-rise made me feel guilty about being a vegetarian. For the first time I saw all life, even autonomous veggies, have a roaring and robust existence if you're lucky enough to visit the beginning of time.

But I needed to eat and Ali hacked a vine with his knife and filleted the skin off the wavy black root and slurped the nectar like a vampire.

"Black honey?"

Gulp "no…"

My recent attempts at casual man-speak or my replications of jack-asses he-hawing around troughs and lockers naked inside the world of masculine envy and intimidation were long since failed.

Andre surveyed a vine for himself and peeled, sucked and swallowed. He offered me to suck but I declined. A shadowed bird springing across the towering canopy perked my head skyward. But the sky was being palmed from our eyes by our mother's damp hair. Like back home, nature reminds you she still considers you a proper animal.

Not one laser of sun broke through the roof's leafy shingles. The floor under the jungle's cavernous big-top emitted a light that gave weight and substance to your sights as in a meditative hallucination or memorable childhood dream. The biodiversity of Congo's bosom is obvious enough but the preternatural spectrum of kaleidoscopic tints and hues that twinkles every fiber of your retina and cornea cannot be underestimated. I felt a general trance gripping tighter the more I tried untangling the optics. Like fighting a potent psychedelic it was a terrible thought so I let the light of nature's church sing me back to my exclusive pulpit.

One second it was all indigo ink washing the scene and in a cut-frame switched to acrid orange like god was fitting the jungle for prison and we're along for the ride. Speckles of magma from the hair-holes of light raining through the roof caused my balance to rift, thinking I was under attack by little red armies of insects massing at my feet. If our mother turns, moans or feels like an unpredictable sleepwalker we wait for the end of her dream and hopefully slip from her skull like a memory from a brain when she wakes.

We waited. Thin skirts whispered and we all rotated to Andre who had spied the tiny natives hiking half-nude towards us. The girl-women and boy-men had little toddler bellies while their elders: men-boys and women-girls, were slightly more disheveled and trodden. But all had dots of natural white paint checkered on their night-skin. Tan-man, being the geeky coward, asked aloud to Ali why they dress like that?!

"They beautify their bodies with chipped teeth, clay like you see there and scarification."

"I believe it's defecation, Al."

"Sure…"

Their nearly naked bodies excited none of us. I waved at their gathering group while they smiled and pointed. They pantomimed at the used vines and Andre nodded behind his crossed arms. Their scent had blended to match the innate odors of the jungle so obviously, this twenty-three thousand mile hunk was in their childish DNA.

One androgynous native stepped to Arthur and offered a hand not extended sideways but raised in a 'stop' gesture.

"I don't want to get any of them sick. They might die."

The person moved inward.

"Go! Get away!"

I asked the only real question that sprang to my life, "Do they suffer from patriotism?"

"No..."

The Pygmies twisted their necks round as one with the spooky connectivity packs of animals use. Two black jeeps with attached tops came rolling down the aged trail. A lone cyclist ahead slowed their speed.

"What the fuck is that Toleka doing?"

This crippled looking native fashioned in crinkled khakis drowned under a mountain of goods; sacks of rice, gold dust, varied bullets, panties, a baby coffin, red metal cans of gasoline and one case of cola. All of him made the two-car procession behind nearly halt and me nearly laugh. No horns were used on him. We eyed and waited for bits of his cargo to clamber to the mud but his multilateral versatility held everything together.

He stopped and parked his cycle using stupefying patience. He plodded toward us as Tiger's men waved to Ali from their jeeps. The Pygmies kindly waited and greeted the Chinese in their abstract gestures. The four henchmen removed their counterfeit shades and warned the Toleka with their glares.

Dress shirts and dress paints made the dubious men seem like a league of secretaries showing up to a jungle instead of a spa. These men held more slickness in their respective hair do's than all of us. There was much more intimidation and gravitation with these men than the five Ali destroyed earlier. Ignoring the others around us the henchmen spoke first.

"Ali."

The lead thug sunk his shades to eye our boss.

"Yes?"

"We need to talk alone."

He went to whisper words in his ear-hole but we could decipher it, "they might be tipping off the rangers. We've spotted them trailing you three miles away so we need to talk about that and the bodies you and your men left behind."

"Did the Rangers find them?"

"Yes, before we could dispose of them. Now they have a trail and it's hard to shake them now that they have natives and villagers helping to find you."

"They're finally getting paid?"

"Most likely."

The Toleka fiddled with his mountain with a glass of cola in one hand, then turned with a dilapidated stance to politely begin his sale's pitch. The Pygmies daydreamed at the woven roots. On the deplorable mud road, Al informed us we were staying the night here with Tiger's men and the next morning we would take what ivory we had back to a plane that would take us to Liberia to meet Tiger. Apparently, Ali needed to discuss new tact's for the hunt with Tiger.

Tan-man asked from a corner of his crooked mouth if we were heading back to the plains. Al said if the Rangers were hunting us we would kill them head-on if they approached us on the trail.

"We'll all sleep with one eye open tonight if they approach. We have the upper hand in the dark. They don't know we're waiting for them. I'd rather kill them here than take a risk on the plains."

Tiger's men parked their vehicles with one facing north and the other guarding the south. No one was traveling this road without our approval until tomorrow. Over one shoulder I watched Al purchase an item the Toleka dug from a tattered pouch.

I asked Andre what it was, "…it might be time for the celebration already. We've never encountered the Rangers hunting us yet."

Somewhere in his skull, a storm of snot sloshed making his speech a bit stuffy.

"You think they just want things to calm down before we begin hunting again?"

Sniff, "maybe. Tiger would want his shipment now if there's too much trouble. We just need to rest and…"

"Recalibrate."

"Yes."

I had the curiosity to ask if he would read my book when it gets published.

"Maybe, I don't read."

"A lot of people don't anymore. Books aren't dying, writers and readers are."

"If you give me a copy I'll keep it." Aww, thanks, smart guy!

"What is he buying if we're celebrating the end of the hunt?"

"A drug."

"What is it?"

"We've been using it once a year after every season is complete."

The tension Al had been bottling the last week was noticeable enough and not to be disregarded as mundane mood swings. His new disregard of me and of the pressurized season being bungled with unforeseen trivialities kept the little dynamite fuse of a vein throbbing on his temple day and night. I hoped he didn't have it in him to crack-up and pop us all with his Herstal in the downfall of it all.

Andre and I shook hands on doing our utmost to satisfy Al and reinforce any new plans he would make.

"We're the best team I've been with. This is the best team he's ever had. He was excited about you in the beginning."

"And I'm sorry for being so naïve and inexperienced. I know I'm a failure and a disappointment, I always have been to everyone."

"You don't have to apologize for trying to get experience. I was lost too when I first hunted ivory. I had to pay attention to my friends to see how they did it and replicate them in my own way. I think you fit in nicely. I would have you on my team. Just because you're not perfect doesn't mean others shouldn't give you a chance or you should hate yourself. Self-hatred is the worst trap we have in us."

And Andre, I am so sorry. If your philosophy wasn't dancing inside a murderer's body I might take that advice for myself. I have to say to all my silent readers that Andre, besides me, was the best among us. Andre, if you snatched a copy of this book please tell me you read it and didn't just use it to impress the whores you paid too much for in your proud house bought and paid for with this experience.

But you're not there, here or anywhere. You're gone just like everyone else in my life and I'll never know what you would have thought or believed if given a crack at my words. You would have believed it all because you smell the truth like a shark sniffing blood miles away. I just hope my readers will have senses as acute.

The Bambinas and Topeka's and other residents that used this so-called road had worn it down to pavement perfection. A road of this primordial caliber is also seen in the swamps and plains of Mississippi and Alabama. But this world that survives by its own laws of impregnable seclusion and patient expansion combined with wizardly rejuvenation would make old Dixie look away forever. Time wove a story too sly and surreal to be explained – that's why I'm here.

My words are all of the delicious pastels that paint the whole picture. They sparkle from my neurotransmitters out of my now numb nails of mallowish calcium then are transferred to chocolate-black ink streams to form visible words - my mind and my pen. And I'm sure you're engagement with my little thoughts couldn't foresee me spinning round 180 degrees clockwise to go, "boo!" at the tiny Toleka trudging back up the path.

The lewd scratching of his sprockets stopped.

"Do you need any supplies, sirs?"

"Don't you have any oil or grease for your bicycle?"

"Ha, it's the one thing I don't have."

"What did you sell that man just now?"

"Drugs."

"Do you use drugs?"

"I use ibuprofen and other medicines to numb me on the job. He wanted some and another one that people like a lot." "What is it?"

"N-Dimethyltryptamine"

Andre announced to me and the trader, "the hunt is over." I swore the trickle of a tear nearly hopped from one of his eyes. My heart both shrank and exploded.

The Toleka, with a will impervious to defeat, ordered in his indigenous accent of the sloppy African nimrod, "I have lots for you to see."

Andre waved him off.

Off he went hauling the pollution of a nation on his broken back for the loot on his singular loop. Ali and Arthur now seemed to be chattering like aggressive relatives on a fateful holiday like X-mas.

Andre asked, tired-eyed, "Do you want to go back?"

"We can't go anywhere else."

·*·*·

The Rangers had taken an alternate route on some forgotten, undercover path none of us knew. The five henchmen rolled up their casual wear and changed our gutted tube for a hard new buoyant all-terrain tire. As the bulb in the sky went from florescent white to lava lamp urine we all huddled to construct plans and strategies if we were ambushed. Three men, two of theirs and one ours (Tan-man) would sit at the wheel of each car: side arms in laps and eyes fully alert. Andre volunteered to stay under the belly of the vehicle with his shotgun fully choked and cocked.

Ali nestled himself with a spare blanket nursing his nocturnal shivers and sweats – poor ailing Ali. All the vexation he's headed to would leave any decent killer convulsing. Reptilian insects paraded outside. Their piercing orchestra rose higher as the night plunged deeper with every tick of the clock. Oppressive chirping, rattling, and lisping, tickled our world. An eerie lullaby of millions of tiny beating wings and tongues sailed me to sleep. Somewhere in the blind carnival I imagined a little proud insect boasting butler jacket and tie kindly waving one of his dead comrade's antennas as a conductor wand.

*****

My little butler conductor flat-lined the entire symphony to a scattered rehearsal by dawn. Tan-man lurched frozen from the vehicle as the jungle warmed itself in its own light. The driver door was ajar and the Pigmies had returned with double their original lot.

Easing forward from the back seat I noticed Arthur dead at the wheel with an open canyon on the nape of his neck showing three naked vertebrates. As I rubbed the night crust from my eyes I studied the clean slashes around his jugular and carotid. Studying further I watched his dead drip down from the car to the dirt. The floorboard was brimming with his blood, steeping his feet to the ankles.

"Hey, Al! They got us again!" Al had woken before yours truly and was conversing with the five Chinese and Andre. The Pigmies had seen the body too and were waiting beside Arthur to hear the verdict. Ali and Andre marched to the Pigmies while I stepped to open my unlocked limbs.

"Rangers?" They motioned toward the jungle.

"Rangers? Rangers?!"

All fourteen brushed back, few retreating before he took the shotgun tilted on Arthur's stained torso and dismembered them with slugs. Few of the children scurried in silence then jolted forward across life's finish line with a few booms. Facing me he snarled, "It pays to speak English."

I must make a quick excursion, silent reader. The following events shuttled at a rocket's surge and if any sort of literary fictionist is even skimming the surface of these little things called words in a compact portfolio of even trim called a book, then they (or you, silent reader) will know that events take on their own lives the second the present disposes them to the ghostly past.

Memories need to absorb like supplements, they accrue mass and effect when fermented in that little vault of flesh generously known as the hippocampus. And my own hippo had to ingest, digest and then finally excrete the excrement of these final events in order for me, your very humble author, to place them in this swelling and seething third world library. In short, I didn't move my pen until our story was at least three months finished.

And here I am, finally using my cackling memory to accomplish my crackling true tale. I love you if you're reading me. Ali fingered the gunk from his filthy beard over the news that Tiger needs to see them now in Liberia at his recently acquired diamond mine.

In goes the fingers, out comes the grime, "gentlemen, I'm sick, I'm tired, I've lost two men and I have rangers hunting me now. Understand when I say I'm in no mood to travel to Liberia now. I cannot complete the entire hunt and I'll do what I can to make up for the lost time."

These men were given more direct orders to be firm with Al. A side swine handed him a phone in-dial.

"Tiger, how are you?" His voice prattled off with the rest of him.

Even my energy bar needed recharging. What else could I do but stare absently in the vacuum of the jungle? How was I even here now?

All I heard was Al yelp at Tiger, "Serengeti!"

Chapter 16

The chubby chump had greenlit a last-second hunt that landed us in the Serengeti. Al wanted to earn as much as possible to make up for the reduced profit. The original status quo was slashed and gutted like a-you-know-what.

We nestled plenty of horsepower, clocking one hundred and forty-five on the coppery range of the Serengeti, but our innate gas tanks would only take us so much further.

"We're out of time to use drones to see everything. We'll have that crate there filled in four days, five. We're getting as many as we see."

"We'll see what we can get."

"Use your gun, not your mouth."

But I knew you can accomplish more without guns than with them. Spattered Acacia trees greeted us after touchdown.

Tiger had shown a kitten's resilience to Ali's sudden request to sack one more weeks' worth of profit, "fish and barrels, Tiger."

Tiger meowed he could aid with a helicopter or two, sitting professionals who would easily take out thirty in one day but without the butcher's Midas touch.

It was not so much a meow as a roar and this time Al compromised, "but don't let them interfere with our hunt. We pick up their pieces and we still pick up ours."

Tiger purred an agreement of sorts. Those iconic Acacia's were pinball bumpers where whole herds of African elephants maneuvered. But Tiger's two low-soaring, unmarked jet rangers did fly by loudly overhead, whipping our eyes and hair with Al shouting Egyptian expletives at their blending metal tails. A jeep was requested again for easier aim and quicker shots.

I hoisted myself on the two low bars on either side of me while Al and Andre gyrated from the lumpy terrain's instability against the vehicle at one hundred and ten miles per hour. Feeling the aftershock of a busted flu he parked forty yards ahead of the family and held the fat trigger of the automatic shotgun. The adults' skulls and legs popped with blood and skin bursts. The children peeped in alarm and Ali chugged them down beside their parents.

The first two families we destroyed totaled twelve members. Al confessed to a stress relieving joy found in shooting the children especially. Al and Andre ate the meat as is after the six tusks of the second family had been allocated under my seated legs. I politely drained a syrupy can of mandarin oranges between slaughters and at the end of the first day, we collected nine tusks from our own venture and fifteen from Tiger's helicopter raptors.

They sent us the quadrants of the remains and we eagerly undug the swords from their mouths. After exhaustion nearly caved us all in forever, we constructed a rude little fire with no visions in sight on the reigning plains at messy dusk. They ripped through pounds of elephant flesh over the fire while I polished my last little can of whole kernel corn. And the idea of money trickled along my mind like so many nickels and dimes.

After this private war, I might be a man with at least six figures, probably more, in a Swiss bank account. But mentioning payment and the future to Al now would be a suicidal impulse on my part.

Al began lecturing with the black scent of burning skin ribboning up my nose like hellish snowflakes, "I love coming back here. It's always good to see an old playground still flourishing. Being here makes me proud. It makes me proud more than a fourth of all the ivory now being sold comes from these hills. I guess it's like a suit walking home to Wall Street."

"Tanzania is pretty so far but it's the Iowa of Africa."

"Do they kill ten thousand elephants a year in Iowa?"

"No, they kill that many in cows."

"But hillbilly idiots aren't smart enough to make a living slaughtering elephants."

"They stick to cows because they're pigs. They love familiar company."

Dry thorns and tawny pins of grass ate into my crossed legs.

"This land is so rich with life that I know other poachers who put animals on jumbo jets and fly them off to where they need them."

The sun crawled on our clothes as it became unborn on the floor of the Serengeti. Darkness pressed it into the earth but left us above. That goblin's gold that waited for me with my new life after this pulpy mess kept intruding on my inconspicuous candor.

Al was tipped by my features, "what are you thinking about now?"

"The ending."

"I'm trying to salvage the ending for us."

"And I appreciate it. We're all doing our best." That's when I discovered silence is the loudest noise in the universe.

Andre began again for me, "I'm taking a long vacation after this … this hunt has been maddening."

His final word hit as a lone bolder in a dud avalanche.

I waited to get Al in my crosshairs after I said, "there's a limit to the amount of madness and violence people will put up with for love, but not for comfort."

"It's also weird how two people can do the exact same thing and the result totally different. You know, like hunting elephants."

"Artists have to cheer for the things they despise otherwise they'd be obsolete."

His meat paused mid-chew, "what do you mean by that, artist?"

"I don't know, I'm exhausted."

"No. Are you saying we need to make new prejudices for art's sake?" His bleary chomping rolled on.

"Yes, something or other."

"Tell me, what do you do with all your thoughts besides put them in that book?"

"I say everyone's imagination is their savior. It's what I look forward to, what I desire and dream of that sustains me, keeps me stuck and damns me."

"I agree. Have you ever heard the saying it's the people with the least to say who talk the most?"

"Did I write that?"

He guffawed with that mashed meat on his single white tooth.

"So, how do you feel after helping us do all of this?"

"After you do a really bad thing it's easy to say it wasn't that bad."

"True."

I gulped the acrid, jaundice juice from my canned corn.

"Do you know what your future holds?"

"I know the future is already written."

"Very good. How do you know again?"

"Because I've already written it."

"..."

"Kidding, kidding. By understanding mechanics, how everything works, you see the future is already written because it's already in motion. If we know there's an ending waiting we must have already seen it once."

"I always said humility is more arrogant than ego."

"Every bit of existence mirrors itself on every scale."

"You must get very lonely."

"Sometimes."

"You'll be able to find plenty of company among women with the check you're getting," but a slip of his diabolical gears appeared in the form of a nudge to Andre's knee.

A joke on me, at my expense – impossible.

"I'm not interested in love or women. For women loneliness is a treat, for men, it's the main course."

"Women are not novels. In fact, life is not a novel; it's not all about the ending. What do you think as a man when you're with someone? Don't answer as an artist."

"I can only get so close to someone. It only makes me feel content that this person is content with me, or makes me feel superior if they're in love with me. When I'm with a lover I think, 'when can I run away and see how I truly feel?'"

Al had opened his laptop and used its camera to pluck elephant from his teeth with the tip of his knife.

"You have to be the saddest person I've met."

"Why do you say that?"

Suck, slurp, swallow, "because you hardly speak and you've done an awful job because despite what you say you're always daydreaming and never paying attention to the hunt. You're always letting us down and trying to hurt us. We'll discuss what your payment will be when it's all over."

"My payment."

"Yes."

"What about yours?"

"I know what I'm getting."

"Do you?"

"Of course. I'm your boss. Would you like to challenge me?"

His hard grizzled body peered at me, challenging like a wise elephant before gorging.

"Of course not. I love you, Ali. Al, you're the only real boss I've ever had and you've been nothing but brave and strong in the face of adversity. Please don't take my stupid words the wrong way. If life has shown me anything it's that I was always wrong until I joined up with you. Joining your group was the first step in a new direction. Bless you, Al."

"Don't call me Al. I hate it."

"Okay, okay."

Andre's dim nod to my complete horseshit soliloquy charmed my truly despicable side. Having a big murderous baby fall for your lies is as heart-clogging as a dad seeing his little one burp their first word.

"To bottle this talk up,"

"I'll say when it's bottled."

"Sorry, I'll put a nipple on it for me."

Should I flee now? Wait, I already wrote the ending a few months back. This is already over.

*****

With our own six eyes, we sighted across this small twenty mile stretch of the Serengeti ten park rangers. They marched single file like fleas along a stained pencil. Al at once flew the drone out, reaching two hundred feet overhead.

"I know these rangers are not trailing us."

Andre raised his rifle to peer inside the scope, "twelve there."

Their tiny army progressed east and west.

"It would take them fifteen or twenty minutes if they had vehicles to reach us. But maybe they're sending some?"

Al slung his shotgun beside me and off we roared north to spy and pry more ivory away. Their dotted bodies faded along the horizon.

Al barked, "twenty-two!"

Andre comforted, "if we see any more ahead we'll kill them for fun."

"Of course!"

Their words sped back in the storm of sunny winds. Forty-five minutes of being fanned by the artificial breeze of unnatural speed and burning alive under the organic nuclear beams of the hot dot in the oceanic sky let my brainwork simmer down, even when I noticed the translucent sacks of sun spots on my now blond forearm hairs. I ruptured one and I had to let the rays cake it to a perfect clot.

The Serengeti's random spots of water, desert, forest, anorexic woodlands and midget grass were traversed by or through completely. Of course, it turned into a safari scene with lions roaming here and gazelles prancing toward life or death with cheetahs eagerly rumpling their spotted shoulders eyeing prey in sight and a new family of elephants.

For now, with no exit in the immediate reach, I distracted myself with the idea rangers would save the day as stricken superheroes ready to kill what's wrong with the species and bravely scurry me to safety after the cinematic shootout. But very naturally no one rescued me, no one cared as always.

Though a tingling did cross my blood over the idea that rangers are around and maybe lady luck won't knife me in the back this time. Maybe, by luck and timing, the Rangers would decimate my two anchors and walk me home on their shoulders? But this is not fiction and honest celebrations only happen in fantasies.

The heroes who halt death and mayhem in its steps have no time for smiles, cake, and top hats – at least not honestly. The best I could dream for was a quick sniper's shot at the two who rummaged inside the bull's head while I cowered at the rear tires pretending to check the air pressure. I was so aroused I could have inflated a monster truck tire on my lungs and lips alone.

A casual clumsiness has always shaded my natural behavior, for instance, as a man always inside or beside myself, never just A-self, I scratch the latex from my thoughts like shimmering lottery tickets to reveal if I won the jackpot of 'the right answer'. Seldom am I in the moment so when someone grills or presses me from around a corner or spins in a line to face me and does the same, I have to concentrate the visuals on my tip-toes to splutter the response for them as Al did, "have you checked the ball joint on that rear tire?"

"…uh…that's, um, not the problem. I, uh, just checked the tire and that's fine. We have to move again to see if it's the, you know, the joint."

Plenty of responses like that occurred during the hunt. The more I was shaken up and away from my natural abstract thoughts the less I gained with my boss. And it only spooled out my insecurities and paranoia over this ending more and more. I already did something to assure I got the ending I wanted but being the watery writer I had to dip and slip through the crunching grip of the man beginning to get thoughts of strangulation.

Now, despite my natural self-coaxing back to dreamland, my toes had to be sturdy and supine as a ballerina's.

"Hey!" Up go my new toes.

"Yeah?"

"Start the car, you're driving now."

I palmed the keys that graced my grip but landed limp and rattling at my boots.

They truncated the tusks before I blew out the exhaust with my foot. I couldn't risk Ali using my untimely key-turn as an excuse to shoot me for 'harming' the ivory. But Admiral Ali only bedded beside Andre as Andre took temporary charge of this evaporating mess. Into my tunneled ears his wet breath flowed: words heating my eardrums as Africa's motherly breaths cooled my lobes.

Al had settled his shades high on his nose-ridge and sat arms folded as a stuffed version of his robust former. The itching fears of his hibernating shell bursting to animation and opening my windpipe a la' Tan-man's nape kept my eyes where Andre's words told to go.

The remaining week rested on this mountain's lonesome ridge. I scraped my heels causing pebbles and dead debris to drop to infinity but my, what you may call 'insane', precautions and reproaches around Ali for the last week of the season kept me alive in my mind. And my mind is all I have unless you're reading this, silent reader. Then you have my mind too, or what's leftover.

Chapter 17

Welcome to Liberia, this is Toe Town! A back-home radiance shook my hand and welcomed me right off the five-step airplane door. The shivering sweat that prefaces illness, exhaustion and death began flooding from my malfunctioning pores. My skin and everything below was going haywire from little food, piles of posturing, too much physical activity and violent overstimulation. The seizures of angst birthed honest visions of me doubling over beside my boss.

If I'm shot or left to wither inside a cannibal country than at least I can finally catch up on some overdue rest – the pillowed, permanent kind. From plane to slick black limousine were thirty or forty forgettable feet to a healthy creature but my own unruly body panted and heaved for its own life when I tried restoring it on the not-cold-enough leather seats. My reflection, my translucent double, stayed slumped and rumpled like dying fruit in the window opposite.

The tinted scene beyond me showed the bare-boned environment of those tarnished mercurial avenues downtown where I walked the devastated streets and teased the nightwalkers at midnight en route to Paradise Liquor. The fog of grey life that permeated back home and now this equally dysfunctional space plopped dirty memories back into me with every rotation of the tires.

Moldering clichés like poverty, pollution, corruption, crime, debt, debris, blight, bankruptcy and death dribbled off my artistic thoughts and natural sensibilities. The only difference, actually one of few, between Toe Town Liberia and back home appeared in the peoples' resigned attitudes. Here, see those children splashing the mud on that half dissolved mule, the unforgivable people show no restraint because they came from nothing better whereas back home we are rooted on a tree that long disposed of our kind and we've since mingled a new grim attitude of past days of glory with a terminal blind daze.

The skies are comparable enough. The frozen junkie I discovered in an obliterated home at eight had more a familial relation to the children serving the human skull as a football over there than anything else I've experienced. Blown out bungalows and burned down buildings either trashed inside warzone concrete or black savage mud played on a loop. I had finally come home again. So, here I am clammy with physical congestion in a newly acquired limousine with chauffeur ahead and boss and co-worker behind.

Through the nail of Toe Town, we curved along its urban cuticle of the main road slimy with swamp dirt. Africa never looked homier. And if diseases like this keep spreading read this novel as a bible if it strikes a town near you. The main road displayed bigger junk homes than Bruno. Each home or business was a homespun concoction of salvaged scraps, the counterfeit fringes of shame advertisements written on stolen cardboard with untraceable paint.

And see those damp black figures strolling in clothes that wouldn't match on Mars? The wise chauffeur vroomed ahead towards the backcountry causing my rioting insides to vault with aggravating inertia. The smug Chinese penguin squawked and flapped in the mud, ruining his webbed dress shoes. The limousine parked on the dry side of the divided earth.

No construction workers, smoking foreman or pricy dinosaur equipment was around. It was all child workers without shoes or proper pants compacting into this ditch, that tunnel or the query beyond the rabbit holes. Like little black insects they scampered and lurched from hole to chasm conferring with each other over their findings. Tiger was maybe half a foot taller than the smallest fourteen-year-old boy.

The teenage group leader was gesturing about a spot over the query and got put on hold when we three drudged up. Off he goes! Throughout the talk, the minute tinkling and clinking of the boys chipping useless rocks for window stones played as an ambient soundtrack. "Well, Ali, there are always some losses in a business venture this lucrative and expensive. It's not the apocalypse."

Another apocalypse, Jeeves.

"You look better. I just began this venture a month ago while you and the boys were still sacking the bulls. I employ fifty kids to dig for me and it's legal. Half of all the kids here drop out of school anyway so I better give them some work."

As an organ to my hometown's funeral I wanted to pipe out loud across to Ali and Tiger, 'ninety percent of kids drop out of school and they don't have work waiting for them.

Oh, and they're all armed. This is a swell little operation you've got Tigger.' The lead lad approached and kindly waited on the outskirts of our orbit to tell Tiger of the progress made.

"Look, gentlemen. This is Coleman." The proud kid faced us, hands in pants pockets. "The future of Liberia, like everywhere else, depends on the youth."

Sturdy young Coleman stood about-face with features etched in virgin stone.

"We don't force these kids to work. Coleman, like the rest, signed a diamond contract in my office under his own supervision. Thankfully, I have the power," and at this Coleman, kid-coma, pouted his proud chest forward with brimming pride, "the governments and their Ministry of Education has only thrown empty threats my way. No mines will be shut down."

The proud penguin clapped his back for him to speak up, to mold his own sale's pitch about child labor being the wave of the future. His soft serious voice mumbled through the uncertainty of puberty, "things are difficult on my parents. They didn't want me to leave the classroom but I had no choice. And here I am looking for the future here. I hope to find a diamond soon."

And here I am, Coleman. My parents needed help too and so did I. Look at what similar situations across cultures and continents do to us. I love you. I myself needed to dig elsewhere than a cavernous child mine for my arrival into the real world. But maybe Coleman and his cronies, not being creative types, will strike a diamond-encrusted escape route brushed in gold and not blood?

But I have a little secret, queue the organ again, time is still wisdom in this book and I have fore-glimpsed the future of certain lives in specific sects to know what a hapless, horrific and ultimately harrowing future lies ahead on that old yellow sick road. There's no diamond encased lottery ticket sleeping for your discovery. There's only you. And you mean nothing to the world, just like me. But you can mean everything inside your own, like yours truly. Kill organ.

Coleman spurt off to his Bambi-eyed underlings while Tiger continued his speech and moved us back to the smoking chauffeur. In a sidewinding gimmick, he casually said, "I just used my own dynamite to blow that crater for the kids." 'What a sandbox!' Inside the slick cozy locust, Tiger padded his twin breasts with both flippers, striking nothing (oh, the fucking irony!) so he snapped for four at his driver. Like an oriental fan of cigarettes, he handed one to each of us. Yes, I'd say I earned this cigarette. My fire gum was long gone so this back home reenactment would suit me well.

This familiar strain of death excavated my lungs again, much like the meat smells of the elephants, as all of Africa swiped inside my inner airbags with a million dirty scythes. The nicotine high, as opposed to cannabis, swelled my skull, placing me unkindly on cloud 9 with the threat of a stroke becoming a more believable reality.

But the pressure deflated and I settled back to my current sickly weight. Tiger swiveled beside the minibar burping busted words like "Good Golly!" as "Gut Collie!" When a river of whiskey streamed down his zipper the crack chauffeur knew that was a signal for slowing. "Tiger, do you mind stopping the car?"

"Not for long though. The children always hope I'll pick them up for the night. They crowd the car." Ali pressed without theatrics, "I want my men to get an eyeful of Liberia. And I want our business to be between us now. They can find some fun around here."

Tiger sipped his fish juice with wandering peepers at Andre and me, thinking of the nasty predicaments we could try here. "Let them out here. We'll see you back at the villa I'm renting down the road and up that hill. Here's my number if you need a ride back." I pinched his eggshell card from one extended flipper. I waved it up to him with a nick of gratitude while lumbering from our seats. The chauffeur parted with one hand erected in a salute from the side window.

Andre's sturdy stance had whittled to a senior's gait.

"Do you know this place at all?"

His face, tired hard structure sagging like the warrior bulls we butchered – their lazy last looks of wise resignation before the bullets, stayed as he shook the world and my question off. The mud road was bunched in by imbalanced garbage structures that passed for local businesses. Like back home, most of these hubs are without licenses and regulations. There is no law there or here to speak of. This is culture, this is freedom.

Look at the toddlers chasing each other with spare road kill and their mixed bones. It reminded me of my own father chasing me around the garage with a hacked deer hoof. I came to find anyone over sixteen doesn't have a decent chance at making money off of their bodies in Toe Town. We entered a purple tower of four stories at the end of the road. A stubborn sign permanently off center and with a terrible surface to stick paint to, read 'Food, Beer, and Lottery' then came its French translation hiding beneath. Talk about homesickness.

Believe in better things here and just wait for the disappointment that would bury you where you stood. To me, it was normal – a more tropical escape to my old hometown. I've waited in a world like this and the inbuilt emotional muscles that grew allowed me to finally arrive here without the effort of flexing. A grey rainbow veiled the smoldering sun. Neat, not bleak. Meat, not feet. How else do you think Toe Town got its ironic name?

The vendors we passed had free samples of three human bodies. And you know the toes had the hometown sauce on their tips that won thousands of blue ribbons like elephant ears back home at the state fair. Or the remains of the pregnant raccoon my dad had hanging by its neck in the basement for me to watch him further annihilate. Out come the babies! No time for foster parents now.

I released my Akwa pen to the kids climbing and gripping us. So goes my only means of translation until I landed securely inside China with Al. Maybe upstairs on the fourth floor, a barouche restaurant flaunted its items and décor but nothing but leaky water crying from the fissures of the place greeted us instead of a Maître d. Voices of children from a left corner playing a peek-a-boo game forced me to see their play.

Oh, the smells were tunnels that expanded in offense with every step taken. The weak dance of a single candle warped the dark walls of the room. And there they are. And here I am. Child slavery, like the holocaust, is just fronts of words. Not many people explore the structure the signs are attached to. It's when you realize you're lost in the wrong building when it's breathing in your throat, do you realize, 'Oh, this is what that is. No one uses a child slave as a butler. Of course, it's about rape – rape for dessert before and after every meal.'

Seeing unwashed children sharing a pipe on a dead mattress made me at once remember the definition of 'child slavery'. Their trafficking tears welled from dead sorrow. It was now an automated condition. The children had forgotten the conscience definition of horror, but the tears kept coming anyway. When they looked to me there was the hysteric shock of too much beastly potential, and Elvis nearly left the building.

But hey, prostitutes are survivors. They confuse survival for living at such a young age it all just becomes survival. And by having to always just survive, if surviving is your job, then everything is allowed. Welcome home. I only asked the girl of about ten if they make good money.

Bashful and high she shrugged to the dead mattress, "Sure." "Good job. At least you have a job. Where I come from a lot of people do this. And we're Americans. The future is very bright for the world." I wanted to tell the terrific triplets how no one will help, no one will care and no government in America, China or other hell will save you for all the land and wealth in this wicked world.

But I kept my trap shut. They know about it all just like me. This isn't rock bottom, it's the mountaintop. I just hope one of them has a bloated artistic strain in their precious DNA like me so they can slip this ship and soar with the other vultures everywhere. Let their lives ring with irony, distraction, and creation. I should airmail them a copy of this when I dot the final sentence. But again, they already know more than you, silent reader. If we ever run into aliens they'll say they avoided us for a reason.

On the third tier of the human-haunted African pagoda, I approached Andre's punctured body nestled in another velvety red room with sleazy paraphernalia. The stabs seemed from a sword or machete. Finally neutered inside his own heroic corpse I'm thankful he was murdered as he desired - a solider.

I saw myself relieving the tiny flame that did a wavy waltz to the low ceiling but a perverse, not superstitious, pang spooked me in the form of his body reanimating in the dark to devour me. I exited with a nod and acknowledging bow of the inept citizen. Mother Nature tinkled on the penguin's card as I dialed his number outside under the forever mourning clouds of Toe Town. The limo-man gave his lazy salute to me again.

The two-mile slide ahead made me want company badly and I almost urged the chauffeur to join my company for a stolen shot at the arctic minibar in back. But we did the impoverished slave's duty of being begrudging, tough and in our world decent. The bird's villa seemed from the one-mile mark designed a century ago by an aristocratic anteater. It rested injured and off center on one side inside its ruddy frame. The foundation had been crippled by the unsteady mound it was rooted in. Beyond was the panting jungle.

After Al heard my news his own remains remained stiff. Tiger clucked a low curse and emptied the stray drink left in the bottle inside a new glass, passing it my way. It was something yellowish I remember. Who knew all of this rotting colloquialism could still be so atmospheric. As Al revved for reaction I toasted to the little ivory elephant statues grieving at tiny headstones. No doubt they belonged to some ironic undertaker's funeral parlor. I nearly toasted, 'Here's to irony, I mean ivory.

The adult silence among people in amorphous and unsteady jobs like elephant poaching, gambling and diamond mining settled down over us, inside the Victorian white room. "Think it over Ali. You still have plenty of money to buy fifty new hunters."

Tiger tipped his drink before it drove down his hatch. Ali, emaciated Ali, bored a horrid hole beyond the desk he faced. He had lost twenty pounds, his eyes slept alertly inside their caves and the old billowy black beard now seemed pasted onto a living cartoon of a terrorist. The bravado, boldness, and balls of this man were irretrievable now. His mouth lisped some remark and we waited until the energy came for his mill to turn again, "I have a lot, I have a lot to think over. When do I get payment?"

"Fly with me to China. I'll restore you personally. I'll have it there in any form you want and you can relax, get healthy again and think about the future. It's not likely I find another ivory dealer that's so reputable and reliable." His strained digits held a stop sign midair, mid-sentence, "look, I appreciate the casualties and hardships you went through. I can only compensate by making my home yours for a time."

Oh, Al. Do you want to go to this beast's home? Who really wants to go home but the dead? Ali's leftovers scrunched ahead for an ill handshake reminiscent of the parting cancer patients'. Despite the testosterone being punctured and drained here I dare not consider speaking out loud, out of turn or whatever else might get me cut from the game completely.

"You two rest here tonight. Tomorrow we'll fly out." The tidy chauffeur rounded the corner to show us to our rooms. I almost held Ali up like my dying grandfather but he managed a rickety rise on his own bones. Heading down the forgotten halls, the halls new criminals buy from the ghosts of old ones, the scarecrow shuffling from here to there before me was approachable intellectually but emotionally I couldn't bother the man, my only boss. In my own obnoxious bed that night I awoke to aimlessly contemplate the hunt. The idea of right and wrong entered me and when I began exploring their definitions the whole continent laughed at me.

Chapter 18

We left Liberia without even our hats in our hands. Something beyond humility had now held Ali for maybe the first scenario in his existence. The crippled and unguarded airstrip appeared round a bend of waking foliage. He had really risen in his seat after slugging shots at the minibar, toasting to farewells and new beginnings etc.

The white baby plane kicked away without delay. His pouring continued in our puffy blue and black stitched chairs, "Hey! Of all the people that lasted! It was always in my head you wouldn't die...man, for being an amateur I picked really to be cheap help and a casualty you somehow clung on, or whatever you did." Sip the stimulating syrup, Al.

"I mean, look at it, you could hardly kill one elephant. They're all so easy to kill. How did you miss? They told me in Bruno you were an exceptional shot with all this experience. But I guess back home is getting softer and less violent." And this was where his voice did a fast nose dive to save decency or regard the new idea at his werewolf bosom.

"Maybe you're getting smarter? Maybe you're crazier though because of how much has changed so quickly, and so poorly. Maybe you're weak now despite all that has changed for you." I began the end with a patronizing head-shake, "oh, Al. Always absent Ali."

"Hey,"

"Hey!"

"…"

The better cobra finally stands. But I sat, with one claw aiming my .1911 at his chest from my cozy seat in all that pressurized air conditioning. The sonic humming screaming to be let in provided the neo-cryptic symphony.

"I'm drunk, but I'm not afraid to shoot in here. I won't miss so put that gun away now."

Tick goes the hammer, in clicks the cartridge into the black chamber, now waits my finger.

"I can't believe you didn't read my novel, Al. I'll let you in on the irony I wove into it but ironically you don't deserve to hear it if you're too lazy to read it let alone interoperate it."

"You can still save yourself if you holster that gun."

"Stop worrying about guns. You're a soldier, remember? You're not afraid of a little death are you?"

"Put it down."

"…"

"…"

"Good. Now. Do you really think those Rangers could find their pricks let alone any of us? I said at the beginning of this I was drawing memories in hot blood, but it wasn't *my* blood…"

I unzipped my duffel with my free hand and located the hidden needle under this manuscript, tossing it on his wrinkled lap.

The remains of his face studied it, "what does it mean?"

"A3/02. It's a super strain of AIDS. See, I took it from the doctor in Bruno – I'm sure you remember the vacationing Santa Claus. When I got the idea the screech my heart emitted was comparable to his little elves shitting themselves with joy."

"What are you talking of?"

"I took a needle full of the stuff and quietly injected you and the rest of the gang with it during our long tired walks. But…I still had to murder them because I'm *crazy and weak*. AIDS isn't quick enough for the world anymore, at least not my world." I shot a prom photo smile, "more cold medicine? But maybe I'm just crazy and weak like everyone else back home? But certainly, there is strength in weakness. And there's intelligence in insanity. And here I am."

"And here you go!"

Click goes his dead Herstal.

"Intelligence Al!"

The final stance of the cornered prey arrived.

"Insanity, Al! Stop trying."

I waved the loaded clip between two fingers like a treat.

"I found out earlier than most are supposed to that death is just another word for the past. Back home in my city, you can get away with murder over and over and over again."

"…"

"Come on, Al. The knowledge of death shouldn't cause fear, it should kill it. Take it like a solider. I don't think there are tragic ways to die; there are only tragic ways to live. I think when this is all finally over for us even our space dust will somehow find each other. I want to know that law. Do you want to know my law for doing this?"

"…"

"Murder is possible once you don't look at it as murder. After enough time passes you look back and say, 'oh yeah, I did kill someone.' It's like an old bad lay. I wanted to kill like a teenager wants to have sex – I wanted to finally come into my own. I wanted to finally be all of me. Somewhere in Bruno, I reasoned it was fine to do it again if I needed to."

"…"

"They say this will all go away and nothing will reign supreme again – that all the power we know of comes from nothing. I guess the Pygmy's were right about the darkness, you know? I guess literature and elephants are already gone. I guess I'm watching the ending already."

"…"

"Don't worry, Al. You won't see the death of your own body, no one does. But hey, even in death we still exist inside life. Killing Andre was the hardest if you want to know. I got him face to face. He died like you will. You deserve that respect. Got nothing to say?"

"…"

"I'll kill Tiger too when we touchdown. I'm a busy man these days. And I knew if I put a little blood in this fifth novel of mine, if I gave it some sensationalism, I would get it published. There aren't enough people now to help novelists or elephants so I had to resort to this. All the deaths I'm accountable for were artful deaths as my readers will attest to. And the ironic justice sweating, heaving and bleeding on the pages will speak to the right people. Still nothing to say?"

The last face he showed me showed the real man behind the illness and alcohol. The eyes of the predator formed into the bulbous Bambi-eyes of the prey.

"You think you will last? Do you think killing is a kid's game? You won't last another week if you keep this up."

Then came the prepping sigh of the condemned, "enjoy the life you have left. We're always one breath away from death."

"You know it."

*****

'Dear Mark, before I left home I murdered my father. Don't stop reading, it's only me. I've always had good luck with bad luck so I've enclosed my novel and a submission letter for you to mail for me. Once you read it I know you'll send it off to the address on the SASE because you're the only decent friend I've ever had and I know you'll want justice to prevail. Here go the invisible symmetries that elude you at your altitude: I raped Rayless.

I hate writing 'rape' because it's been misused and abused like everything else. I read her correctly like I do everyone else. And what did it do for me? What did I get out of it? I saw she was the female version of me and we both sniffed it out silently. I knew she would let me rape her, and she'd like it.

That's why she laughed at me before I began. But something tells me the world has always been laughing at us, and we laugh at each other and at it out of insanity, music or fear. Did she tell you? No? I was right about that too. Pardon the terminology but nothing goes deeper than that.

She wasn't the complete demon I am but she hoped and fantasized she was. She just wanted to hope her quiet fantasy into a loud reality. Like what I did as you'll find in these pages. Only we were both predators and you'll always be the poor scapegoat – the sad prey. I guess that's why I wanted to love you so badly.

I guess that's why I'm leaving this bloody manuscript in your water bowl. There's not an ounce of predatory marrow in your skeleton, even if you think there is, there isn't. Trust me, this is a predator speaking. And Mark, you're the only decent person I've met because of it.

I hope you'll still help, to give to life, unlike me. I'm still hedging the ugly shrub I see every day. I know all of this because I'm not a middle-class college boy, sorry Mark. I had to explain about Rayless for your sake. Women don't understand love like we do. If women really knew what a man's heart was all about they'd fight to get it reclassified as a form of mental illness.

I hope this paints a deeper portrait for you: all of this. I now consider myself a survivor, and as we all know: survivors are the loneliest people. Empathize and commit some skullduggery on humble me. Being a writer, an artist, gave me two ways of reasoning, two ways of acting and two ways of being. There are two sides to everything. The grey area is just a waiting period. Things either happen or they don't. Laws don't break, they mingle and reflect; the hunters/the hunted, creation/destruction, life/death, black/white, me/you.

I'm still lost and alone on this only-planet. Mark, I'm tired of being tough. I'm tired of being sensitive. This was my only out. The world bows to bullies and now a few sinister victims and it's still not right for me. I've been a bully and a victim and I hated both.

The tipping point that snagged me in life was believing, even for a millisecond, the teachers and other bullies were right – that my dad was right in hating me all along. Am I just worthless? Am I not even worthy of a minimum wage job? Quitting my last job back home made me consider, 'if I'm going to embrace art (escape) one more time I want to contort its corpus. If everyone hates me then I'll be the best at being hated – easy enough! I won't concede to being wrong and I won't concede to them being right – fair enough!'

Before I left home I gave a wandering black kid ninety dollars of my dying grandmother's money so he could raise funds for his 'academy' to have a football team. I told him to eat the candy he would've given me. Sweaty, skinny and sorry he told me of the people who told him to get the fuck out of here and the other racist swine who abused his ambition.

He came to me at the Woodward Avenue Bar (how ironic!) and I pitched him his share and more. He and I had comparable lives though his father had a better job than my butchering loser of a victim. I'm not all bad and in fact, I relayed some life-hacks I've hidden in these pages. His honesty shined after his bowed silence kicked by me like a lost kitten, like myself and every other victim back home, for a whole hour.

Embarrassed he shook my hand incredulously before I left. This, my only friend, is proof of my goodness opposed to the murderers I ran with. Whose worse – the serial killer of elephant poachers and butchers or the rule-abiding racists who clog society's arteries with covert ramifications? The kid, who slipped about being held back a grade, saw through those clowns who rejected him. Much like I did with the publishing business.

But he couldn't see through me – the real decent devil that gives good luck on bad days. That kid was me in so many ways and showering him with a dying Nazi's gold proves my decency. If he bought drugs with the money, which I consider because I'm the evil complexion of ivory, I still did the moral thing because I gave a chance at escape – the way my father handed me the lone dollar to buy the pen to write this bloody thing before I ended him.

And here I am telling you how good I am etc. I gave back; once more than most of us do, to the helpless. As do you with Bruno. Love me? Marry me? Forget me, like everyone else.

Love has been so bad to me. Literature has been even worse. And no one has empathy for the author. No one cares novels come at a real price. Just like money and toys – cover your eyes! Like back home – what happens when you neglect people and entire cities, entire states and whole countries? What happens when people neglect their village, their neighbors, and their own lives? What happens when life becomes a throat-cutting race that's judged by superficialities and not humanity?

I think my own story, right here, is a fine start to an explanation of the tragedies we cannot hide ourselves from. I can honestly reason anything through desperation. I have for a while now. Just like my brothers playing in the sand not too far from here, always sprouting new groups to deal with hell through violence.

Do you think I have any confidence in life, in myself, in anything but death and suffering? Do you think I believe? But Mark, mark my words, the best mindsets rise from hellish lives. I can be the happiest bastard I know. So what does that say about the virtues of your morals and decency, your college, and debt?

I've always been tastefully damned and for that, I've always been damn tasteful. I don't know how these things happen but some people are born to live alone or with others. I don't care to know the reasons anymore, but I'll go through all of this alone…that's why I'm a writer. You better pray or cross your fingers there's some justice for me because I will pay you a visit in the future if you don't mail this out and help get this masterminded manuscript on shelves around the globe.

Of course, I would never hurt the ones I love. But they will hurt me, keep hurting me and finally kill me in the end. Is that justice? I don't believe in the idea myself. Justice is another word for getting caught. Just like how luck is the word we use when the chaos favors us. And what will happen to my kind when we're gone?

Since this package doesn't have a return address it might not be read and I'll be rejected again; my love and my life. I guess because of luck and timing I was always meant to do this, fulfill my game-life from the moment all this absolute determinism was banged to life light-years ago. My dad never knew he was helping to birth his own death. And my boss and co-workers didn't know they adopted their own deaths by getting into this holocaust before I ever appeared on paper.

Ah, this messy paper. All lies disappear and never withstand time but if they get a good hold they just get piled into more colorful lies i.e. religion, but the truth is finally running that down too. And literature is the most impressive lie of them all – count all the bibles in history and their influences for a tally.

But I'm tired of lying. I'm allergic to pretension. I'm afraid of collusion. So who's going to know who I am? Who's going to believe me? No one really reads anymore. Literature has no serious place in the future. And a guilty man can't be caught if there's no audience, I mean evidence. Literature is going the way of the elephant.

Even with it all written down, it – I will keep moving unnoticed. Just like the novel, elephants and death itself…I'm dead news. I'm already history. And your all-American doll-of-a-dad stuffed with raisin testicles, sappy sports shirts, moronic muscle cars and proudly unused hair dye bottles should not haunt your innate ambition with love and life. Don't mimic his life by letting a fat, all-American wife clutch your bitch throat with an expensive leash on loan from your weaknesses. Though you have a more disappointing father at least he wasn't a butcher. If I can escape in my own way, so can you.

What I really got away with was freedom. Only in a place this free could I do this much damage, just like back home in the land of freedom. I have to savor this position. I don't need encroachment or rules. No more dumb schools. Away with ludicrous laws.

But when I'm extinct, when I'm gone forever, who will replace me? Remember, there are only the hunters and the hunted – the predators and the prey. And there I was - I was there. And there I went - now I'm here. And here I am – now I leave.

The orgasm of art comes to me now in a vision of strangers' eyes roaming a zoo full of books and spotting my exotic cover behind the bars of a price tag, guarding the cage bars of my words. Silent reader, if you're still out there hearing the last faint bleeps of my colorful signals I have to scream one final communique: my words appreciate your hands! Thank you for holding me until the end.'

Thank you for reading this book by Motor City Press, an imprint of Mad Hatter Publishing, Inc.

Keep reading for a sample at David Ryal's next book, *Not Tonight*, due out next summer. For updates on David's books, short stories, and gifts as well as announcements and updates about his next book, head over to his website and sign-up for his newsletter at **DavidRyals.com**.

If you want to find out about all our writers and their work, our giveaways, launches, and more, head to our website and sign-up to get all the latest on your favorite authors at **MadHatterPublishingInc.com**.

Thanks and keep reading!

NOT TONIGHT

BY DAVID RYALS

(SAMPLE)

Chapter 1

(A Son Settling on a Setting Sun)

To: Mom
Subject: Not Tonight
Date: Saturday, June 20th

"Mom, you were right. I promised I'd keep my promise and tell you how this is turning out the second I landed. But before I tell you what happened last Tuesday night I want to say I love you. I don't know what to think of myself now. I now exist somewhere between the dead-end wall of eternity's spooky tombstone and last Tuesday night.

But I don't want you seeing me any differently and worrying about me. Last Tuesday night I ventilated all of my steamy spirit into a woman's mouth. I've already gripped regret and it slipped from my clinch like a foggy ghost. I'm not coming home because, like I said before I left, I'm also here to find my new life.

I know I have to help myself now, but how can I get treatment for an illness of fiction? I met her at a small dance club. She nailed my shoulder with a finger,

"Do you mind if I sit with you? We can pretend we're in Europe for a minute."

Now my k-9's are not fangs (yet) but I know I have this condition after our night together.

I know the most mysterious and important part of our body is DNA so I don't think it's too abnormal to crave drops of it so consciously now. DNA is life; in its vast codes is the mystery and power of human life. I see the craving for what it is now. Please tell me if that or any of this sounds crazy. I don't eat anymore, I'm pale as cheese, I'm still broke and in piles of debt.

Last morning I peeked at a few sunbeams splitting through the curtains and it felt like I was holding my face too close to the stove, like when the heat scares your skin. The razor still swipes my sunny hairs away but shaving at midnight is weird, but whatever - people always get weird after midnight. I'm getting used to my night being day now. I know we don't always turn into what we want in life. And often we unknowingly predict our own death, but what happened last Tuesday night was extremely lame. It wasn't what I predicted or wanted.

Since I landed in this town, beside a major city that's fighting for a new image, I should fit right in I guess. There are touches and tinges of Jamestown here. I've heard the country here is a lot like upstate back there. I'm hoping I'll find my niche on this notch of the rustbelt eventually. Now buried under a glacier of homework and thrill and shrill of immortality I've got a lot more to figure out than anyone else I know.

I have about ten hours a night to unwrap the tethers orbiting my brain; is there a cure? Will anyone accept me? Where can I work? How can I become successful? Where can I make friends and contacts? How can I network? Again, please don't worry. I'll manage to live my new star-crossed self until I find a productive routine I can live with.

Before I sleep for the day I'll give you a quick sample of what my life's like now: last night when I was walking the trees screamed and swarmed with bats every time I passed underneath. They love bouncing images of their human counterpart off of their little ears. Nine Mile is Ferndale's main street and last night all the shopfronts were comatose. Even the cars stopped sparkling under the parked stars.

When I realized romance was a hologram for me now the bats flapped and squealed two blocks down. Somehow we both know what we feel, my understanding is just bigger. That's all I can tell about our relationship now. A lot of the storefronts have 'Help Wanted' signs in them but they're not open at one in the morning. I'll figure it out. Some of the neighborhood bats left a couple of dead rodents on the sidewalk under the trees for me when I was out walking. But like an unspoken bond between pet and master they shied away when I looked at them and said, 'really?'"

***

To: Jonathan
Subject: Tonight

Date: June 21

Jonathan, just because you think I'm right doesn't mean you're wrong. My main concerns are not with you believing you're a vampire (is that right?) but with your new identity crisis. Anyone you sleep with can suck more than fluid from you and I'm feeling that's what happened. Please tell me more about her: this steamy woman who ventilated your spirit.

Your education comes before anything at this point in your life. As a teacher and journalist you know I have to reinforce my convictions regarding my life's work and deepest beliefs to the person I love most in this world. I do believe you are overwhelmed by the move and the one night stand. But as a mother I need to be your guiding light until the sea sweeps you away from my lighthouse, when I will fizzle and fade from reality but not from memory.

So let's objectively calibrate your situation and the events: you just moved from home to a new, very gritty city. A woman preyed on you and under the pressures of leaving everything familiar your heart is no doubt volcanic right now. You have always wrestled with school and it's a handful to achieve anything real inside its structure but all the effort, all the investing, will pay off after you graduate and achieve your potential inside the world of journalism.

Don't worry about the money. Money has nothing to do with success. That is the first illusion you can discard that will alleviate stress. Your tuition will break away from your engine as you climb higher and higher towards your scattered stars. I won't go on about your rigid and passionate view of public education. As I've said before, public education was my investment in your character for you to conquer your struggles.

You always saw yourself the way public education saw you. If I judged myself the way public education judged me I wouldn't have any confidence in myself either. Yet here I am. As a writer I'd like to know more detail about Detroit and the nice little city you're tucked away in (Ferndale). When you were accepted to Wayne State University I was elated and I still am. Forget the University of Michigan and Michigan State.

Traditional universities aren't the tea in your cup and you'll be healthier for it. We've always traveled on the humble highway and you'll need to exercise your peasant's spine to accomplish the real dirty work needed in the world. Now concerning bats, blood, fangs and sun scars - I hope you know you're not a vampire.

It wasn't Dracula's bride that rattled your nervous system and made you a fidgety insomniac. No vampire bit your neck and made you Nosferatu. I know, because I'm your mother that you're peeking over your laptop and stretching your neck over both shoulders only because massing fear has finally pooped on you to make you paranoid about life itself.

I will always remember you as a kid rotating in circles when something pulled your senses, like a kitten chasing the ghost of its tail. I miss your sunny hairs and peering blue eyes already. I'm a mother and I make no apologies for embarrassing you with affection. Go out and run in the sun. Make having coffee at that little cafe a cozy routine to help you unwind. Only in college did I discover the magic of coffees and their houses.

If you are going to be a professional journalist you will need to replace your appetite for blood with caffeine. I had no idea Ferndale was exotic enough to have trees teaming with bats! Please promise me you will make notes of them and not friends. Give me a quick list of the businesses there, I'm very curious to know the structure of the city.

Call or text me when you can. You know I do enjoy the written word so I don't mind if we keep the talk fluid, rich and vast with emails. I love you. Stay strong, stay my son and sun. Who cares if you turn into a bat? Don't forget we're all animals already.

***

To: Mom
Subject: This Weak Week
Date: June 28

Mom, your colorful wisdom raised me well but I feel in my bones that the crossroads I'm at now, and will forever be at, leads me to Nowhereville. Like Jamestown, Ferndale is Nowhereville. And now that I'm hexed by one of life's endless curses I don't know if I can keep moving backward and pretend it's forward. Being a vampire seems to be the runny cherry on my life's sundae.

It was never your fault we weren't as rich as everyone else, but I know you think it is. I got that from you - I think everything is my fault. I've searched for jobs here and the best I can do is restaurant gigs that pay less than minimum wage. Did you ever think you'd end up raising such a loser?

The jobs here are for eighteen year olds who need weed and gas money. Given my new state I don't know that I can focus on school or waste what little time I have at night with a joke job. Juggling vampirism is not what they make it seem in books and movies. Entertainment keeps lying to everyone about this condition. But I think it's fair to note almost everyone in my generation looks to entertainment for guidance. Kids base everything on entertainment because they have no experience.

What I'm saying is I don't know how much longer I can go on like this without seriously considering saving for a gun and putting it under my chin. But of course! A bullet won't even stop me now! Wow. I can't even begin to believe this. If I decide to bail I'll have to do it the most painful way conceivable - burning alive.

I never thought the sun would become my enemy. Matthew is in Los Angeles and then he's going back to New York City, then down to New Orleans again until Halloween. He said he didn't want to come home to Michigan again because before he left to house-sit in LA he said living in downtown Detroit was the worst time he's ever had living in a city.

I'd only tell you, but when I read his texts and emails my blood boils with jealousy. He tells me not to be 'jelly'. Of course I try not to be but seeing my best friend forego college and get so much traction with just taking off on his own makes me envious and massively sad about my current position. I'm twenty three and I've already gotten such a late start with higher education that I feel it's a rat's race and I'm the only one in the maze.

Everyone else stands above with pens, clipboards and white coats. It's my own private hell. Of course I hold the keys to escape but my pockets are too deep with debt to find them. Writing to you helps. It's my only release from this curse. Anyway, I've vented enough to worry you for a century and now I feel horrible for making you horrified.

Ferndale is fabulous; at least that's what the city's corny nickname is - "Fabulous Ferndale". But nothing is fabulous when you have no money. Everyone knows each other and the others are just visitors.

The apartment you picked is okay. It's above a pastry shop and the sugar-scent invades my little back window if I leave it open during the day. I've been sleeping with it open because I love the fresh air and I'm hoping the hot smells will invade my brain and make my dreams all pink and purple and yellow.

I want anything but crimson on my mind. I'll tell you how I'm dealing with the cravings I get for blood and everything red. It's kind of like when we quit smoking together except there are no blood patches or blood gum. I suck on change to help and it works, thankfully. Pennies taste the best.

Anyway, Ferndale is different than Jamestown. When I'm not cluttered with school work I'll write more about it. I do know it's a city that needs to be discovered on your own in order to understand it. It's not like New York or any other place Matthew has been or is going to.

I can see the potential for it being fabulous but I'll keep my eyes open at night for any fabulousness. Oh, I switched all of my classes to online classes and I do all my work at night which cuts down on my free time but whatever. I need to study for a test coming up and saying that sounds as hollow as the inside of my apartment, indeed this new ghost-life I'm in.

Tell me how your students are. I want to know who are the most interesting, the worst and the best etc. I guess I don't need to say you need to keep paying my phone and internet bill until I find a job. I'll keep looking. I love you! And I'm sorry if I scared you at all with what I said.

***

To: Jonathan
Subject: Bats, Rats and Races
Date: June 29

Jon, first off get those pennies out of your mouth and take them to the bank, and not the blood bank! All cool people start out as losers. Remember the old saying 'winners are just losers who never gave up'. Eventually everyone sees through everyone else and the only ones who pull any gravity are the ones who give a constant, unattainable effort.

You have opened up to me at your lowest about self-confidence and not being taken seriously. Self-confidence ranges from a tight rope to a suspension bridge. Take my advice and don't look down right now.

The thing you'll have to get used to is having the guts to tackle emotional subjects objectively. That's a sweet idea on paper, I know. But let it bloom inside your brainwork. Once you see into someone you can see through them. And you need to start with yourself.

The rules were made before we were and we just have to play along. I can honestly say last year's class was a memorable and colorful one but none will compare to yours, when I could be the crutch you needed.

We have touched on the subject of love many times and I know you well enough to know you will not make me a victim of your own death. As much as your sadness leaves you in the dark (yes, pun) I don't want you believing death will eventually be the answer.

Death is temporary, only love lasts forever. And remember, if you can't take love seriously than you can't take life seriously and that's where it all goes wrong.

Only lonely people can be cool and you're alone just like me, so don't worry about that either. Don't think of dad's tragedy now. It will just fan your flames more. We share the same blood because of him and we're tied together until the world whirls to crumbs. That's the beauty of family.

I want you to try and settle into Ferndale in a manageable way - deal? I love you. Keep me updated on your happenings and don't fret over the imaginary. Over half the stuff in our head is static anyway. I love you, especially tonight.

Mom

***

To: Mom
Subject: Foretelling Ferndale
Date: July 3

Mom, I have had a few days to digest my emotions and I've readjusted to my new night-only schedule pretty well now. I seriously appreciate you trying to help but I don't want any more drama in my life given what I'm going through. The fact that you don't believe I've changed and are trying to make colorful commentary about it is hurtful because it feels insulting. I don't want to hurt you with that but that's how I feel given my condition.

I liked your thoughts on suicide, though they seem a light year from pertaining to me right now, but I really appreciate your insight and it did soothe me a little. I was feeling my fangs along Nine Mile in the downtown district last night and I've noticed they're a little sharper. I haven't peered at Ferndale during the day obviously.

I did take your advice and went out (with only two quarters in my mouth) and mingled with some of the bar hoppers and night hawks. I've switched to quarters because they don't taste as bloody and I'm hoping to ween my appetite away from blood all together but we'll see. Quarters taste like diet pennies, like the pennies are gluten free, sugarless or non-gmo (something less bloody and more healthy). I went to two restaurants and got a couple drinks: a whiskey at Cosmo's and two Bloody Mary's at Impractical.

Judging by last night the crowds were mostly hard working hipsters looking to get plastered to cope with their lives. It's appropriate I join them I guess. The big wooden patio at Cosmo's was closed so I scrunched into the packed wooden bar and watched the reply of the Tiger's game.

No one is as friendly here as they are in Jamestown. Everyone here is in their own world. I could take the bus to downtown Detroit but I'm a little nervous to go there, plus I'd like to familiarize myself with Ferndale more until I'm comfortable enough to go downtown.

I didn't really get to talk to anyone; just a few people said "Hi" and left me alone. Thankfully my new condition has probably made me immune to alcohol because I didn't wake up hungover. Despite how flat last night turned out it did spark my appetite for more of Ferndale and I know I'll spread my wings and find the city in my own way among the luckless crowds.

That's when I really want to spill my mind about it. There's a big art market on the corner of Woodward Avenue and Nine Mile called the Dust Belt. Its windows are lighted up by all different kinds of lights that showcase the mess of displays. I'd love to explore inside soon.

Thankfully they're local artists and desperate so they're open until midnight. Some people were roaming in the parking lots by the bars. As I walked along I heard through the low clouds the blending claws of jet engines thundering the ice-black stratosphere. Eventually I found myself alone on Nine Mile in front of The Red Book Cafe. It's open until two like the bars and I wanted to go in but I was pretty buzzed and had no money left for coffee.

I just went home and tried doing some homework for my history class. But when I go out again (maybe tonight) I'll tell you how it is. Basically there are restaurants and specialty places like vitamin shops and cell phone stores. Mostly it's restaurants and bars though.

Are you doing anything for the fourth? I'll miss the fireworks but I've read about some displays happening around here in some cities so maybe I'll get a drink and go see a show. Anyway, I have to get my homework done. I want you to know I'm feeling fine right now so don't get too worried. Matthew's been texting me so I'm happy about that. He'll stop by and visit in a couple months so I'm really looking forward to that.

I was researching funeral homes that sell coffins but I don't have the money and don't have a good enough story to really get one so I'll keep sleeping in the closet. It's actually cozy and just dark enough. Have a nice night. I love you. Now tell me about your last class!

***

To: Jonathan
Subject: Independence Fray
Date: July 4

Jon, I won't tell you how to live your life at this point. My concerns are you missing out because of fear - hiding in a closet cannot consume your days! You know by now I don't believe you're a vampire but I do believe fear is dripping from you pores like a shivering marathoner. That's the crux of your condition: fear.

Most people are afraid to be themselves because of rejection and you have faced your share of it. We all do. You always complained about being a child because you had no freedom. I was the same way.

So don't feel awkward now. Ignore being awkward and know everyone else is too. See awkwardness for what it is - the natural mask we use to handle action. What I worry about (remember I'm a mother so I make no apologies for worrying) is your rationalization of fear: your rationalization of superstition. That's how racists and ghost hunters stay in business.

Don't let your emotions run your intellect sweetie! Open up and don't believe you can do it all on your own. You need to be flexible, not solid. We need to be able to be soft in the hard places when necessary. Know that decency is as good as currency. Don't ever forget that.

It's a sentiment I try to impart to all my students. I'm getting so preachy because I know fear is made of ignorance. I see it every day in the classroom, and outside too. I've preached enough for now.

But fair warning: if you don't stop your vampire monologues I'll come to Ferndale and drag you outside in the sunlight and destroy your fear! As a teacher who's taught you and countless others English for thirty-five years I recommend, in fact urge with all my esprit, for you to begin a journal and work your anxieties out through that.

Hell, if it turns out to be high quality writing and insightful enough I'll read it to my English class next year with your permission. Tell me how the Red Book is. I'm sure you can find someone there to reach out to in person. Start observing your own life like the journalist you want to be. I love you!

Mom

More titles by Mad Hatter Publishing, Inc.

From our Minerva Press imprint

Narcissistic Abuse – A Survival Guide by Sara Teller

Ms. Teller brings to bear her life experience combined with her intellectual and academic studies and presents a thorough reference book addressing the differences between healthy narcissism and Narcissistic Personality Disorder (NPD). Three distinct and separate sections focus on:

- Narcissism as an inherent humanistic trait versus pathological narcissism
- Victimization and the healing process
- Therapeutic intervention

Dark of Night by AM Paoletti

A gritty thriller/romance based in Detroit, MI. A terrorist is planning something big in Detroit just in time for the President's visit. Antonia "Toni" Andiamo discovers it's the same man who captured and tortured her in Afghanistan, the same man who ordered her family killed. She's on a mission of revenge. Dealing with the a Federal Task Force, FBI, an "unofficial" CIA agent, and an attractive Special Agent in Charge she chases her enemy, knowing that time is running out.

From our Expansion Press Imprint

Billy of Flawn by Sammy Ogg

Inspired the by death of his young son in 1976, Sammy Ogg - a child actor in the 50's and 60's - takes us on a fantastic journey with Billy as he finds himself in Flawn, a kingdom in another dimension for children, after he's struck by a car. His guardian angels, Cypress and Hollyb, tell him that Elohim has a plan to help all the children of Flawn and has called Billy to leave earth early to carry it out. You'll discover Billy's purpose and follow him as he fulfills Elohim's request and takes all the children of Flawn with him.

From the Brink of Suicide – How an 11th-Hour Revelation Made Her Put the Gun Down by Adrian

This is a true story of neglect, abuse, and a life-time of depression leading to one fateful night when suicide seemed like the only option. Sexually assaulted by an uncle at a very young age, she was ignored and then sent away when she tried to find help from her parents and other adults. The scars left behind tore through her life leaving her teetering from depression to mania. Doctors and medication were of no help. One night, with a gun in her hand, she came face to face with her inner demon and found that she had the power to banish him. That night, she wrote the main part of this short book, "In Search of the Emerald City".

Choosing to go only by "Adrian" to protect her children, we learn about her early life and the trauma that caused her so much pain. Her message: depression is only a fierce demon until you choose to chase it down and confront it. Once you find your demon, you have the power to banish him for good. There's no promises made, no panacea, but her life continues as an example to others who struggle with depression and thoughts of suicide.

Publishers Note: This manuscript was found in an abandoned storage facility along with other remnants from a now defunct publishing company. Somehow, it found its way to our offices and, through some digging, we found the author. We were moved by the story, the plight of the little girl and the struggle of the grown woman. If you've ever been touched by suicide, this book will shed some light. If you've ever contemplated suicide, this book will be very familiar.

From Sherwood Press

The Fabulous Feats of Mr. B by Bruce Weinberg

Mr. Bruce teaches children about creativity and imagination. Using relaxation and breathing, he takes his kids to a place that's peaceful and serene. Whether it's the top of a snow-capped mountain or a sun-drenched white sandy beach, Mr. Bruce transports your children and you can come along, too.

Try it at home, anytime, to help your kids relax and expand their imagination. Just have them close their eyes, inhale ten full, deep breaths (from your nose to your toes) and take them to any serene, picture postcard scene.